Master: How large is the universe?

Herrin: How long is a string?

Master: Should our world, Freedom, concern
itself with space?

Herrin: The universe is irrelevant: the possibilities of Freedom are as infinite
as the possibilities of all other locations in the universe.

Master: Should Freedom concern itself with
Others?

Herrin: The only meaningful concern of man
is man.

Hugo Award winning author

C.J. CHERRYH

has also written:

DOWNBELOW STATION
MERCHANTER'S LUCK
THE "MORGAINE" TRILOGY
THE "FADED SUN" TRILOGY
THE PRIDE OF CHANUR
SUNFALL
HESTIA
SERPENT'S REACH
PORT ETERNITY
BROTHERS OF EARTH
HUNTER OF WORLDS
THE DREAMSTONE
THE TREE OF SWORDS AND JEWELS
VOYAGER IN NIGHT
FORTY THOUSAND IN GEHENNA

WAVE WITHOUT A SHORE

C. J. Cherryh

DAW BOOKS, INC.
DONALD A. WOLLHEIM, PUBLISHER

1633 Broadway, New York, N.Y. 10019

FIRST PRINTING, AUGUST 1981

3 4 5 6 7 8 9

PRINTED IN U.S.A.

I

Man is the measure of all things.
—Protagoras

Freedom was one of those places honest ships avoided, a pleasant world of a pleasant star, but lacking a station at which ships could dock, and by reason of its location on the limb's sparse edge, inconvenient for ships on fixed schedules.

A few outsiders came here, pirates who were afforded a shuttle landing, and who therefore restrained themselves from their habitual destructions, preferring to charge exorbitant prices selling what on Freedom were rare goods. There were occasional free merchants with similar larceny in mind, but there was also a strong likelihood of *meeting* one of Freedom's piratical clients in the neighborhood, and that prospect discouraged most merchants of any category. Freedom was moreover a poor world, in outsider reckoning. It had grain and preserved meats and vegetables. That attracted the pirates, who had no world at their disposal and needed such things; it did not attract much trade of other sorts.

There were inevitably the military ships, who came pursuing the pirates on one of the occasional campaigns for order, whenever the pirates had gotten too daring and touched off a hunt, or when the powers which ran the Alliance decided it was time to hold a military exercise.

Freedom had no ships of its own, not since the original, which had once been intended as an orbiting station, but which had finally, through disuse and failure of its maintenance, broken up in a spectacular display over the Sunrise Sea. Freedom had assets, sunny skies over large land masses,

5

abundant population both indigenous and human—a condition completely contrary to Science Bureau regulations, since they mingled without safeguards. There was in fact no place on all of Freedom where both human and ahnit could not in theory mingle unchecked and without expectation of violence, a condition superior to that of some worlds under Science Bureau management and control. Freedom possessed broad, moderately saline oceans, reasonable weather with rainfall in convenient places, an oxygen/nitrogen/carbon-dioxide atmosphere with replenishment by vegetation, a vegetation which incidentally furnished inhabitants a minimum of ordinary difficulties with natural poisons and allergens. Tides, under the benign influence of the large single moon, bathed white sand beaches and thundered majestically against basalt, jungled cliffs, sufficient to have inspired poetry in the deadest souls. Humanity thrived on Freedom, multiplying at a rate sufficient to give the main zone of settlement, on the curved, many-peninsulaed continent named Sartre, a very respectable shuttleport city, Kierkegaard, with industry and manufacture sufficient to supply the needs of the farmers who ploughed Sartre's fertile plains. Freedom was almost totally agricultural, virgin abundance well-suited to man (or ahnit), and its lack of trade was no handicap to the economy.

But even the pirates refused to go outside Kierkegaard's port area, and the occasional military personnel who paid official visits to the Residency and the First Citizen, went and returned as swiftly as possible, staying to modern Port Street, which tall firebush hedges screened from the rest of the town.

Curiously, Freedom was not a notorious world, not, like Gehenna II and some of the limb's other plague spots, a breeding ground of legends. Those who had visited Freedom had no wish to talk about it, indeed, tried to ignore it as thoroughly as ships avoided it in their courses.

It was not that it was a place where humanity failed, or where men lost their souls to the strangeness of aliens.

Freedom was a mutual failure.

II

Instructor Harfeld: What is truth?
Herrin: Whatever is real, sir.
Instructor Harfeld: What is reality?
Herrin: Whatever the strongest thinks it is, sir.
Instructor Harfeld: Who is that, Herrin?
Herrin: Here? In this room?
Instructor Harfeld: Of us two, who is stronger?
Herrin: You're older.
Instructor Harfeld: Does that make me stronger?
Herrin: Right now it does.

Herrin Law thrived on Freedom, young, well favored by nature, chance, and the powers which governed the world. "He's gifted," the instructional supervisor had visited the Law household to say one night: Herrin recalled the night with perfect clarity through the years, the amazing visit of a man all the way from the township of Camus, to their bare-boards farmhouse in Law's Valley, where he and his father and mother and sister had been gathered in their town best clothes to see this caller, who had come all the way out from the township to report the result of his first tests. "He'll be University material," the man—citizen Harfeld—had told his parents. His parents had cried a little after the visit, as if it were some kind of disaster; but during it, citizen Harfeld had patted him on the shoulder and congratulated him on a talent so rare that Camus could not possibly nurture it properly. . . . "He'll have the taped courses, to be sure," Harfeld had said, "up to appropriate level; there'll be a government stipend, all the best for such a special student. An educator searches a lifetime for such talents—rarely finds them." So Herrin had swelled up with a seven-year-old's vulnerable pride in himself and understood that he was some-

7

thing different from anyone else in the house, so he was
already able to look at his parents' reaction from a certain
distance of that specialness. His older sister looked on him
differently, too, and seemed to shrink after that special night,
casting furtive looks at him, jealousy and perhaps a little self
doubt, which increased over the years, and cast her in a new
role of second sibling despite their sequence of birth. She developed a whole new bearing after that night; and so did he.

He loved his family, from his slight distance. He was capable of being wounded when his parents petted his sister Perrin in a different way than they did him. He clung to the
consciousness that he would be leaving and that in a way he
had already left them; and Perrin because she was a walking
wound, and she was the one who would stay with them into
their old age. Perrin was duty. She tormented herself with her
inferiority; she lost all confidence, and bestowed superiority
on others who had her about them. Perrin was uncertainty
and self-doubt; Perrin clung; and Herrin, after that night of
the visitor, was simply separate, understanding the position
his precocity enabled him to enjoy as virtual outsider. That
this was the price of superiority, that the same height from
which he looked down on others and analyzed their feelings,
also obliged him to live removed from the run of humanity.
He grew up extraordinarily handsome and more graceful
than his agemates; grew up with a sensible reserve which
made it possible for him to associate with agemates less ma-
ture and less self-assured than he. He was confident of his
merit and basked in slightly lonely love, loved in return from
that height at which he lived; and tolerated jealousy with the
understanding that those less favored had to have *some* defenses. He was kind because no cruelty had ever shaken him
from that plateau on which he lived, since that momentous
visit. Love poured up to him, and he rained it down again.

III

Perrin: *I hate* you.
Herrin: *Yes. I know.*
Perrin: *You want* everything.
Herrin: *Yes. I do.*
Perrin: *That's not* fair. *What do* I get?
Herrin: *Take what you want from me.*
Perrin: *How?*
Herrin: *Just do it. Be stronger. Take it.*
Perrin: *How?*
Herrin: *(Silence).*

He felt pain when he parted with his family, seventeen and
bound for University in Kierkegaard. They cried, even Perrin, but his parents cried because they were hurting at losing
him and Perrin cried because. . . . Perrin's tears were more
complex constructions, he thought, jouncing along in the
leather seat of the Camus bus over the dirt roads, and eventually over the smoother road on the weekly Camus-Kierkegaard run. Perrin cried for herself, and that she saw a
chance departing which had never been hers.

They would all be happier without him, he reckoned, leaning his head disconsolately against the window brace and
watching the cultivated fields roll past the unwashed windows. He had been too strong for them, and despite all the
tears of various quality shed at his parting—the wound would
heal now; Perrin might blossom in her share of the sun, a
belated, slightly twisted blossoming, to be sure, but it was
possible now; and his parents could devote themselves to their
more comfortable offspring and he—*he* could draw breath in
a somewhat wider room. That reasoning did not entirely cure
the loneliness, but he was used to separation in all its aspects.
He did not, with the confidence he possessed, brood over-

9

much on other possibilities. He would not choose to be anyone but Herrin Law, eminently satisfied with his fortunes. He had seen Perrin, who was popular, and unlike Perrin, he understood the reason of her popularity, and he was too kind to explain it to her: he simply congratulated himself that he was *not* Perrin, or anyone else he had met in Law's Valley or in Camus, even citizen Harfeld, who, from his almost adult perspective, was considerably diminished, a rather sad man who sought out and encouraged an excellence which Harfield himself was not competent to comprehend—a useful job, but a depressing one.

Herrin created. He had discovered in himself an aptitude for art; and while he pursued the literary and philosophical and musical studies the school of Camus had promoted, his real joy was in form and substance. He worked in clay and in stone, finally settling on stone as his greatest love, work with old-fashioned chisel and more modern tools, with ambitions still greater than his young hands could yet achieve. He had, boarding that bus for Kierkegaard, left every item of his art behind as inadequate, incomplete, a provincial past to be forgotten along with every other taint of his upbringing.

If anything frightened him at this stage it was his own power, his own intellect, which was in steady ascension. He realized that he was dependent on such as Harfeld, educators of less than his ability, who yet possessed the experience he knew he lacked.

He knew that he could be warped, even destroyed, by inexpert guidance, like some machine of vast power which, set off balance, could destroy itself by its own force. He knew that he must analyze all the help that he was offered for fear of being misdirected; that he must, in essence, *train* those who were to help him in the proper handling of Herrin Alton Law, and that mere good intent or worldly wisdom in those about him was not sufficient, because most people were not capable of comprehending the logic on which he functioned or of comprehending the abilities which he felt latent within himself. This made him uneasy in going among strangers . . . not the strangeness itself, because he was perfectly confident that his own grasp of a situation was superior to that of others, and that, if anything, it would be a relief to be safe within the environment of the great University, where he could reasonably anticipate that his instructors might be more competent to direct him and that his companions—perhaps a few of them—might be strong enough to withstand his strength at full stretch. He was just generally cautious.

He feared . . . that Kierkegaard itself might be a disappointment, that perhaps nowhere in all Freedom was there a place of sufficient stretch for him, and that somehow his self might still fray its edges at the limits of what Freedom could offer. He was young; he was not sure that the universe itself could contain him.

He got off the bus on hedge-rimmed Port Street, and walked the short distance to the University, which was, like the Residency near it, of sufficient magnificence compared to Camus to reassure him. He registered, received all the suitable authorizations in his papers, and settled into the very comfortable apartment the government allotted him.

IV

Senior Student: What do you see on the streets of Kierkegaard?

Herrin: What I wish, sir.

Senior Student: Are you aware of things you would not wish, Citizen Law?

Herrin: I am aware of everything I wish.

Senior Student: You're evading the question.

Herrin: I'm aware of everything I wish to be aware of. I do not, sir, evade the question.

Senior Student: That is a correct answer.

Master: How large is the universe?

Herrin: How long is a string?

Master: Should Freedom concern itself with space?

Herrin: The universe is irrelevant: the possibilities of Freedom are as infinite as the possibilities of all other locations in the universe.

Master: Should Freedom concern itself with Others?
Herrin: The only meaningful concern of man is man.

Kierkegaard was a city growing according to plan, now three hundred years old and acquiring some sense of time. There was of course the Residency of the First Citizen, Cade Jenks, descended from the original Planner of Kierkegaard. In that long, five-storied building the government was carried on, and the planners had their offices and facilities. There was the University, mirror image of the Residency and next to it on that section of Port Street which lay within the city limits. The rest of Port Street extended to the shuttleport, the mostly disused facility which interested Herrin only in theory. MAN, the inscription over the Residency's main entrance proclaimed, IS THE MEASURE OF ALL THINGS, and it was humanity which wanted attention, not—not whatever was outside. Freedom itself was on its way to what it might become, and it had no love of the outsiders who came intruding on its search. The port was, like those who came in through it, irrelevant.

There were ten streets in Kierkegaard itself, exluding Port Street, which everyone did. The central street at a right angle to Port Street, beyond an archway and footpath through the firebush hedge, was called Main. Two vertical streets ran on either side; there was a central east-west named Jenks with two laterals paralleling it, and a paved commons where Jenks and Main intersected: Jenks Square. Warehouses, manufactories, apartment houses, all production and residence fit, completely mingled, within the geometry of the City Plan; an apartment might stand next a mill or a manufactory next a warehouse. The port's near edge was the site of all small trade, in a daylight market. Of construction, there was great regularity: a company in Kierkegaard turned out building slabs, all concrete on a meter of the upper section and a meter of the lower, and covered with river pebbles on the middle; there was one completely without openings, one with a warehouse-size door; one with a double door; one with a single. There was one with a window, a meter square. Out of these the whole city of Kierkegaard was built, with such conformity that it seemed all one building. It was an eye-pleasing coherency. Only the port escaped it. It was a city without ornament or variance. The whole world lay at its vulnerable beginning. Its greatest minds were being brought from all regions of Sartre to assure the right beginning—and Herrin Law was part of the program. He surpassed his instructors; he gazed on the void regularity of Jenks Square with a proprietary eye and the sobering consideration that the artistic expression of a planet lay under his young and guiding hand, for he knew that the blankness in Kierkegaard which was meant to be filled with art was his arena, that *his* work which would one day stand there—he was sure it would—would influence the total of artists to come in Kierkegaard. He knew that if it were great, they must either imitate or react against what he chose to do, and that therefore he would, more than those in the halls of the Residency, shape the reality of Freedom.

His reality, imposed on a forming world.

His self, extended over all the globe of Freedom, because there was talk now of going into the other hemisphere and the continent of Hesse. His work would go *there,* as well.

It was a thriving city, with vehicles coming in from all the Camus River plain, and going out again with raw materials converted into needed goods. It held thousands upon thousands of residents, who passed—afoot—in its streets. But Herrin did not form associations with the folk who came and went in the streets of Kierkegaard. The important ones he met at social gatherings at the University and the Residency; the unimportant went their ways in their own and limited realities, reminding him much of those he had associated with back in Camus Province. He brushed past them on his trips through the city, noticing with simple aesthetic satisfaction that the run of people in Kierkegaard were better dressed than those in Camus. That there was prosperity here, fit his sense of what Kierkegaard should become.

There were more Others, too, which one might expect: a great city was like a magnet for drawing things to it, and like a great machine for producing debris of broken parts. There were those who were mad, or defective. It was debated in University what to do with them. It was early in the history of Freedom, so it was deemed enough until the ethical dilemma was resolved, to allow the defectives to resolve their existence in their own reality, which existed principally at the shuttleport, at night, and rarely in the city. They were the Unemployed, the invisibles; they were excluded and in abeyance. They were inconvenient, but not greatly so. They were not greatly . . . anything.

And more than these—the primary Others, midnight-robed, who stalked through the streets of Kierkegaard mostly by night, with their own purposes, in their separate reality. Herrin was almost trapped into staring, for they were a sight he had never seen; they avoided Camus. But he recovered himself and pretended he had not seen, which was the only courtesy that passed between human and ahnit. It was their *modus vivendi*, mutually practiced, separate realities, neither contaminating the other. Presumably the ahnit gained something in Kierkegaard, but a sane man did not speculate on something that was not human, not in aspect, not in manners, not in art or logic or in any other respect. They left humans alone. It would have better pleased humanity had the ahnit stayed out of human places altogether, but there had been ahnit on the lower course of the Camus obviously for a longer time than there had been humans, and it was a question of prior occupancy. Realities in Kierkegaard overlapped, perhaps, but a little schooling in the courtesies of the city made it possible to walk a street without remarking on the dark-robes. They had nothing at all to do with man, or man with them.

V

Master: What is man?
Herrin: Man is irrelevant. My own possibilities are as
*   infinite as the possibilities of all other beings.*

Herrin *enjoyed* Kierkegaard.

"Living here," breathed Keye Lynn, who was one of Herrin's pleasant associations in the University, "living here is Art in itself. Imagine the effect. We're shaping ten thousand years."

He thought of this, lying in Keye's bed with Keye's body delightfully filling his arms, and experienced a cold moment when he thought that Keye was an influence on *him*. From that moment on he abandoned trust of anyone, suspecting that Keye, who knew herself less talented than he (they were both artists, Keye in ethics, a more abstract field than his), meant to use her art to warp him from his absolute course. It set him to thinking much more widely, analyzing all his associations past and present for possible taint, suddenly aware that there were people whose motivation might be to *use* him, knowing his brilliance; that they might, robbed of their own hope of consciously warping the future—lacking the personal scope or talent for that—yet might seek that effect by using him, who did have such scope and talent.

It set him back for a time. He lay staring at the ceiling in the determination to have that matter sorted out, and resumed his relations with Keye in a new understanding which he kept entirely to himself, that now that he was aware of the possibility, he could do that to others—seize them, warp them to suit himself, that he could sculpt more than stone.

He could widen his effect on the future by being quite selective in his relationships with others at the University. He could gain vast power in many fields by seeking out talents of great acuity but less scope.

Like Keye.

He was grateful to her for that thought. Like Perrin, Keye did not understand him, simply because his reach was wider. Keye would see only a part of Reality, and yet she was brilliant in ethics.

He sought others, became far more confident and outgoing than before.

But the loneliness was there, which Keye could not fill. He experimented with others, who might, by providing him new situations, confront him with new ethics, but his own Reality still encompassed them all, and his own ethic belittled theirs.

There remained Waden Jenks.

VI

Master: Does the end justify the means?
Herrin: What is justice?

"I should feel myself threatened," Waden Jenks said to him. Waden was an acquaintance of Herrin's twentieth year, when some of the graduates of the University were separated out and returned to provincial tasks, out in Camus and some of the remoter areas; or to preparatory work on the expedition which should set them on the way to planetary domination—but Herrin was not one of those so condemned. He was entering on the second phase of his University existence, not as instructor but as working artist. He had an apartment-studio in the University itself, and Keye was there as well, holding seminars in ethics, and Waden Jenks . . . remained. "I'm obviously of moderate talent," Waden proposed to Herrin over a beer in the Fellows' Hall. "I'm obviously here because I'm Cade Jenks's son, and it's my father's wish that *I* become First Citizen after him. I should properly feel threatened by all you brilliant students. No instructor would dare set me down; that's why I've gone on and poor Equeth, for instance, has been shipped out."

Waden was drunk, but cheerful in his self-estimate.

"Evidently you're exercising a subtler talent," Herrin judged. "Strength is a talent."

Waden chuckled. "So is flattery."

Herrin flushed. "By no means. I simply state a fact: strength and possession are primary talents, not necessarily creative but of great importance. If you were weak your father wouldn't throw you into the den of so many predators, would he? Or if he had, you'd have been pulled one way or the other by one of us and swallowed alive. After three years others have left and Waden Jenks remains at moral liberty

16

with all his former strength; ergo, he has not been swallowed or diverted. *That* evidences a talent sufficient for survival. What matter whether you get marks by skill or by intimidation? Intimidation is the manifestation of your talent."

" 'Not necessarily creative.' "

"Perhaps your father intends, by thrusting you into this medium, to inspire you to creativity."

"You're remarkable. I say that freely." Waden leaned across the mug-circled table and jabbed his arm with a forefinger. "Do you know, Herrin, I *am* strong, stronger than my father, strong enough to say that and to know that he daren't take exception to it. I am intelligent, more than he, and again, I can say that. Frankly, most of University is beneath my abilities. *You* know. I think you do. You know what it is to live with wings cramped, knowing that you'll break all that's around you if you really extend them. You have few friends, and you dominate them. *I* am the same. I always have been. There's not an instructor you haven't terrified with your talent, not a student here who doesn't resent you—truth, even Keye—who doesn't subconsciously recognize what you're doing to him and yet find himself powerless to stop you. You're the rock against which most of the University sea crashes. Truth."

"You're talented, Waden Jenks, and you're constantly deprecating your own abilities, which makes you a liar, a slave, or a coward."

"Which am I?"

"Liar," Herrin said with the arch of a brow. "Because subtlety is a part of your talent for control. You are yourself capable of flattery; you flatter me. And of being invisible as the invisibles themselves. You are hated, because you stay here and others don't know what your talent *is*. You're the one they've never devised a class to instruct, but you take the whole University for your classroom."

Waden smiled and sipped at his beer, gestured toward him with the mug and set it down between them. "It *is*. It was created by the First Citizen to be that, do you see?"

"To gather sufficient talents together to provide a classroom for the heir to the State."

"Exactly so."

Herrin was thoroughly amazed; the possibilities ran at foundation level of all assumptions in the University. "By gathering the greatest minds and talents in the world in one place, under one set of instructors, under the eye of the First Citizen himself—and by the shaping of those talents—"

"To shape the course of the world."

"And by observing and learning them, to *know* potential rivals—"

Waden's grin became wider and wider. "Most exactly. You don't disappoint me, Herrin. I thought you would understand when your suspicions were jogged. I am delighted."

"And I am in danger."

"A key to successful manipulation is the dispensing of information. Had you stumbled on this thought unobserved, who knows what actions you might take? I am in potential danger. Hence this conversation. Do you feel threatened?"

Herrin sat back. "So you thought that I was on the verge of discovering this for myself."

"You have been steadily approaching that point, yes. I shall surmise, Herrin, that right now you're more than threatened, you are offended."

"I reserve judgment."

"It's an observed fact, is it not, that when adults want privacy and peace they dismiss the infants to the nursery, shut the door on them; that there's a certain amount of juvenile development that has to take place on that basis."

"The University."

"My father knows the hazard I am to him. Knows my talent, although when he began this project he was willing to have seen me destroyed, had I been weak. Indeed, the University he created would have devoured me—had I been weak. Had I failed, he would have selected the most apt as his successor."

"Myself, perhaps."

Waden laughed, picked up the mug, gestured with it before drinking. "I have no doubt it would have been you, none. But do you know, the older I grew, the more my father was certain that eugenics in my case had paid off. Oh, there *are* failures, a dozen little bastards farmed out and totally useless . . . I'll never threaten them because there's no need. I could swallow them whole. No, the older I became, I'll wager, the more Cade Jenks realized the sensible course was to occupy me. Had he seen to my upbringing, I'd have devoured him. No, instead, he sent me to the nursery—to University, collected this entire den of ravening and powerful intellects and set me out in it naked and unarmed but by wit. Survival of the fittest."

"So he has no prejudice for or against your survival."

"None. None. He simply wants to keep me here as long as possible, because on the day *I* emerge from this chrysalis, *his* existence is threatened. He knows that he can't keep power away from me. For one thing because of our kinship and my access to the Residency. He'll surrender his office, being pragmatic and having a strong wish to live. Indeed, he's intelligent enough to know that the world will benefit from the exchange, that the wisest course for him is to provide me the benefit of his experience and to step quietly out of my way. But that's in the future. I'm only beginning to do that other thing which the University makes possible."

"To remove rivals?"

Waden shook his head. "I *have* no rivals. There's not a one here I can't manipulate or intimidate beyond any possibility of harm; I know the University. Those stupid enough to despise me . . . are the most easily handled. Pride is useful only with those whose opinion we value, is it not? I don't value theirs. No, I'm gathering forces. Persons whose talents are not rival, but complementary to my own. You, for instance, an artist. Do you know, Herrin, that you are the one person in University to whom I shall admit these things frankly? You're the one mind, the one being who *might* rival me, if our talents were not, as they are, complementary. You create. Your supposition is correct, that my talent is not creative; so I seek out one which is."

"No. On the contrary, you've simply delivered yourself to *my* search, Waden Jenks."

Waden considered a moment, and his eyes danced. "Oh, marvelous! This conversation is worth all the years in this dreary place. Do you know, for the first time I feel I'm talking *with* someone, with a mind quick enough to answer me."

"And you wonder if you can manipulate it."

The grin became wider. "Absolutely. Ah, Herrin, Herrin, you're a delight. As you're wondering can you use me, and which of us is likely to survive. I have native advantages."

"Indeed you do. Which argue that I should go cautiously. Likewise there were contradictions in your arguments that suggest a silent assumption."

"Were there?" Waden's smile was ingenuous.

"What do you suppose of me?"

"That you have ambitions. That they're artistic in foundation, as anything would be that passed through that intellect of yours; but that they may not be limited to the creation of superlative statues, the inner vision made exterior, no. You have a very strong reality, and the grasp of a generalist. So am I, a generalist of sorts. I know how to respect one."

"You are a superlative generalist. You do what I do, but having captured the vision internal to each field, you store it, against need. And you will have power, Waden, indeed I believe it. I know that my talent doesn't lie in political manipulation."

"No, indeed, your hubris surpasses mine."

"Philosophy argues that hubris doesn't exist."

"But it does. There are offenses against the State."

"I purpose nothing against the State."

"No, your ambition is far greater."

"Then you know what it is."

"I know. It's Reality itself, isn't it? To impose your internal vision on all of Freedom. Herrin's reality. Herrin's perceptions. I believe you when you say you were searching. That you plan to use me. And I you. We balance one another. If I let you loose, if I let you perceive these things in your own time, Herrin Law, you might ally with some lesser talent, and you would either steer that talent against me, or you would be warped out of your true possibility. I offer you more than any other could: to be at the top, to have full scope for your ambitions. That's the business of a good ruler—to see that the best and strongest function to the fullest. I shall give you what you want; and you'll provide me the security of knowing you aren't inspiring some secondary talent to rise against me. That's what to do with complementary talents, Herrin, give them scope."

Herrin sipped at his beer; his mouth was dry. "You recognize what I am and confess you mean to warp me to your purposes."

"What, so little confidence? From you; I'd expect you to say that you were satisfied to know that you could bend *me*. After all, I'll be the State. And shall I not be one of the subjects you mean to influence? Teach me art, Herrin. Isn't that what you want, after all? Here I reveal to you all my defenses and you refuse the entry."

"Oh, of course, I shall trust you immediately and implicitly."

Waden's brows lifted, and then he laughed. "Of course you will. That's the trouble with my field; every amateur feels entitled to practice my art, but who would have the temerity to walk into your studio and pick up a chisel, eh?"

"You have a sobering manner of expresion, Waden Jenks."

"My art has the disadvantage that no one who sees it can trust the shape of it. I can lay hands on the beautiful marble flesh, and find the outlines."

"But if you believe it's flesh, you've been taken in."

Waden grinned, and then went sober, his brown eyes and thin face most serious. "I *like* talking to you. And that's a motive. There's a feeling of finding someone at home when I'm talking to you, Herrin. And that is *rare*. It's very rare. You know what I mean. Keye is possibly the third greatest mind and talent at the University, on all of Freedom, most probably, because previous graduates don't rival the two of us. Keye's mind is amazing. And yet, can you talk to her—except where it regards ethics? And even then, don't you see things which she would not be able to take into her reality?"

Herrin turned the mug in a circle, until the handle was facing his hand again, studying the amber and crystal patterns on the wooden table.

"Are you never lonely, Herrin? Even with Keye—are you never lonely?"

He looked into Waden's eyes.

"I am," Waden said. "Loneliness on a scale you understand. Keye—has you. And me. Keye has two living minds greater than her own, two walls off which to reflect her thoughts. But our scope is more than hers. There are thoughts you think she can't comprehend, connections you perceive she can't grasp, because you have explained all the pieces of them, haven't you, and she still doesn't see? No one does. Not the *way* you do. But I guess them. I can talk to you, and you to me. Do you know what frightens me most in the world, Herrin? Not dying. Discovering that I'm solitary, that my mind is the greatest one, and that I'm damned to think things beyond expression, that I can never explain to any living being. Have you ever entertained such thoughts, Herrin?"

Herrin found nothing to say, not readily.

"I think you have, Herrin. And how do you answer them?"

"By crowds. By crowds. Three or four pitted against me—can entertain."

"But satisfy?"

"I have my art. You're right, that I can lay hands on it, that it gives . . . presence and substance. Yours, on the other hand, is far more solitary. Whoever sees it will not admire. They *fear*."

"Unless there were one to complement me. One who could take my art and put it in breathing marble and bronze, who could make me *monuments*, Herrin, who could provide something that would not be feared, but treasured, who would make my works visible. Complementary, Artist. I provide you subject and you provide me substance. And we *talk* to each other. We communicate, as neither of us can communicate with others, in our own language."

"How can there be trust?"

"That too, I leave you to discover. Solve my dilemmas, Artist. Lend me vision and I lend you power to spread that vision."

"You don't yet have that power."

"But shall."

"And is power shared?"

"Dionysus." Waden chuckled and drank deeply of his beer. "And Apollo. You are Dionysian and I Apollonian, urge and logic, creativity and rationality, chaos and order. We function in complement. Adopt your protégés. I have my own. We are opposite faces of one object; a balance of forces. Beware me, Dionysus, as I am wary of you. But cooperate we can—and must. The alternative is sterile solitude. We shall beget ideas upon each other. We shall contend without contending, by being."

"I reject your analogy. They're old gods, and we are both of us half and half. Our contending is potentially more direct."

"But the manifestation, the manifestation, Herrin, isn't that the important thing, because there's no way my Apollonian art can have dominance over your Dionysian one save by inspiration; and yours similarly with mine. Inspire me. I defy you to do more."

"When I defy *you* to do more, I fear you can."

"Then have you not, Herrin, met your master?"

"Then have you not met the thing you say you fear most?"

Waden stared at him a moment, then all his expression dissolved in humor and he poured more beer from the pitcher, poured for Herrin as well. "See, I'm your servant. I must be, because I have a need, and you are that need. Without Dionysus, I become stasis, and the world stops."

"We are both Dionysian, and drunk."

"Drunk, we are soberer than most will ever be. No, we are still in complement, because our opposite natures are on the expressive side, and our internal realities are therefore opposite. We are a doubled square of dark and light, complete pattern."

"Then, my complement, *give me Jenks Square*."

"That is your ambition."

"That is a step toward it."

"But I'm only a student." Waden held outward his empty hands. "Who am I to give gifts?"

"Waden Jenks."

"That I am." His laugh at this was different, sober, conscious. "I shall give you the Square, Artist, and you will make me visible to all of time. Visible. You're right that I live like the invisibles, and I don't savor it. Give me substance. Whatever you need, that I'll give. . . . Ah, Herrin, respect me."

"Fear *me*, if I'm your outlet to the world; your substance flows through my hands."

"I've told you what I fear. What do you fear, Artist?"

Herrin frowned, and looked him in the eyes and grinned, lifting his glass. "Your art can't function until you know that, can it? You open your mind to me, that's one thing, but to open mine to you, ah, that's another."

"Marvelous. O Artist, I tell you I find no pleasure greater than this, to find a mind to answer mine, a recognition passing all other pleasures. I ask you no more questions. What you want—is possible. Indeed, you'll find it's possible. Begin your work in your mind; I'll give you the stone."

Herrin's heart beat very fast. He was drunk, perhaps, but only half with the beer. It was Waden's intoxication which infected him. He believed, and that night in his own bed, alone, for Keye had other business, he still believed, and began to build the plans he had already made—bigger, and finer, and more far-reaching.

He had his means. Waden Jenks frightened him, for he knew himself, how dangerous he was in his own power, and he believed that Waden Jenks was at least second to him, in a way that Keye could never be, for Keye was tunneled in on a very narrow reality and Waden Jenks—had scope. And intelligence.

And worked in different ways.

There was nowhere in the University or in the Residency that one was likely to discover the handiwork of Waden Jenks; Waden's work was silence, was subtlety, the warping of a purpose; was kinetic and impossible to freeze. Herrin thought of capturing this in stone, and began to despair.

More and more it became his obsessive concern, the thought that this Man, this potentiality against which all Freedom was measured, had an essence which defied him.

VII

Master: What is matter?
Herrin: Appearance.
Master: What is the validity of appearances?
Herrin: Whatever value I set on them.
Master: Are you not also a manifestation of the
material universe?
Herrin: The universe is irrelevant.
Master: Are you then relevant,
Herrin: I am the only certainty.

He went out into Jenks Square and considered the foursquare blankness paved in all directions, stood on the bronze circle which marked the center of Kierkegaard and therefore of all civilization, and tried to envision Waden Jenks, turning on his heel to the bewilderment of those passersby who must recognize the somber Black of a Student, and therefore a purpose which was higher than their own or a talent which exceeded theirs.

The conceit amused him. He laughed aloud, and spun, and finally in the spinning world about him, conceived the image of Waden Jenks, a frozen form of many dimensions, embracing all the square, an element, a structure inside which all the citizens of Kierkegaard must pass in their daily affairs. It would be a sculpture of monumental proportions, a Reality through which others' Realities must pass daily, until their courses were diverted by it and their minds were warped by it and it became like Waden Jenks himself, so subtle an influence it would distort minds and attitudes without the subjects' being aware, and impose terror on those who looked on the whole and recognized it for what it was.

He walked the ten streets of Kierkegaard, omitting his classes; he looked on the exterior of Kierkegaard, the beige and gray of the solid citizens, the workmen, the sellers, the manufacturers, the occasional midnight blue of one no one saw.

His reality. His visions. And Waden Jenks, captured in stone, apertures and textures and surfaces shifting as one passed *through* them.

He went back to his studio in the University, locked the door, stayed and sketched and planned, mad with the vision.

VIII

Master: What is more real, my reality or yours?
Herrin: Mine.
Master: How do you demonstrate that?
Herrin: I need not.

"Come out," Keye pleaded with him through the door, and to someone else, outside: "I think he's gone mad."

He laughed to himself and kept at work. "Call Waden," he said. "Call Waden here. This is for him."

And Waden came.

"Well," Waden said, "Artist?"

The clay lay before them, the three nested shells which he proposed. The central figure, lifelike, emerged out of a matrix of similar apertures and texture within the dome. He waited, anxious, enormously vulnerable.

Waden walked about the model on the studio table, bent, looked within it. A smile spread over his face and his eyes lighted.

"Everything," Herrin ventured, "and everyone . . . must flow through it. For all time to come in Kierkegaard."

"Amazing," Waden pronounced, and grinned and clapped him on the shoulder. "O Artist, amazing. Order the stone. Select your apprentices."

"What, *now?*"

Waden looked into his eyes, and a curious smile, a subtle smile, sent a slight chill into the air. "I shall move into the Residency soon."

And the week the stone began to arrive, moved by truck from the quarries, to be set in the Square and in the studio, First Citizen Cade Jenks died, of causes unspecified.

The coincidence occurred to Herrin, if to no other. Herrin went very soberly about his own business, matter of factly shut everything down for the three-day mourning and memorial, and very quietly resumed when the public ceremony was done. In fact the mourning was official and very little private, a condition more of uncertainty than of grief, mutterings and wonderings what manner of person this son was who assumed—*assumed* the power of the State, but no one had an inclination to prevent the assumption. At least no one *heard* of anyone who did. There was no disturbance; the Residency remained as mute as ever, as inscrutable. Waden Jenks sat within it. Nothing else changed.

IX

Master: Is art reality?
Herrin: Art reflects reality.
Master: The reality of the artist or the reality of the
subject?
Herrin: (Silence).

The work began in Jenks Square. The five hundred apprentices and laborers alloted to the work began to consider their plans. The voices rang in the dead silence of official mourning, echoed off buildings draped with black.

Herrin stood amid the square, now ringed with stone blocks on which the foundation shapes had been plotted, himself experiencing a drawing of his skin, a sense of the power of his beginning creation, which was Waden Jenks's self, Waden Jenk's reality, the first layer of stones, the first courses of all three shells and of the central pedestal. In his mind he saw what should stand there one day, and shivered.

Waden came on the morrow, no longer in Student's Black, walked about the ring of white stones and acknowledged the respects of the apprentices with grave nods of his head. Of a sudden, Herrin thought, Waden *looked* like power. There was nothing obvious; the gray brocade and conservative tailoring was nothing more than a very wealthy citizen might wear; but the eyes seemed to miss nothing, to linger, invasively.

"With so many hands," Waden said, "you should make rapid progress."

"The image," Herrin said, "is alive in my mind. With the excellent equipment, I can make it flow into the stone. I've apprentices sufficient to work in shifts; lights will keep the work going through the night. I reserve the central image for my own hand. *That* is the focus. In the flow of *that*, the whole begins."

27

"I must sit for it."

"I shall need you to sit for it, yes."

"Did I not promise, Herrin?"

"I think you went rather far in getting me the Square, First Citizen."

Waden chuckled. "My reasons were complex."

"Undoubtedly."

"Do you flatter yourself you had something to do with them?"

"Do you say I didn't?"

"Does it trouble you, Artist?"

"Ah, no." Herrin turned and regarded Waden with a cool eye. "I don't believe in karma, my friend. It's all one to me, whether you acquired your power by abdication or assassination. It doesn't intrude on my Reality. Mine lies in the future; yours is present. Mine is length and yours is breadth." He laid a hand on the block nearest, cool, fractured marble from the quarries up the Camus. "This is my medium. Practice your art, First Citizen, and don't take up the chisel."

"Now which of us deals in intangibles? This stone of yours—becomes *me*, Herrin Law; and my reality—isn't that the subject?"

"True, First Citizen."

"Then where is yours?"

Herrin smiled. "I'm content. The more you're visible, the more I'm there too, First Citizen."

"I was always Waden to you."

"You are whatever you want to be, aren't you? In a few weeks you'll begin to see things take shape here. Those amorphous heaps are the central pedestal, the median arch foundations, the three shells, all the first courses. The first five go into place and the carving begins."

Waden walked further, walked back again. "You'll come to the Residency," he said. "You'll live there what time you're not working."

Herrin lifted a brow. "In the Residency?"

"What, is your self-confidence lacking?"

"Not in the least. I'll accept it without comment."

"There's inferiority in the word accept."

"Possibly. I admit it."

"Now I suspect you of arrogance."

"There's inferiority in arrogance. It assumes one cares. I'm simply as I am. I'll come to the Residency. It seems adequate for my comfort."

"Pathetic games. You're my guest, my employee."

Herrin turned a cold smile on him. "I'm your immortality. Your interpreter."

"Mine. What other message goes out, Artist?"

"Black and white, an interlocked pattern, lovers inextricably entwined."

"Ah, I've discovered your reality."

"You are involved in it."

"Does it occur to you, Herrin, that I'm using you?"

"Yes," he said, leaving pregnant silence, staring into Waden's brown eyes. He smiled finally, as did Waden.

"If you *were* master," Waden said, "you wouldn't have to argue from silences. But you must."

"I don't contend in politics. I argued that from the beginning, and the power you have is not mine. Since you lend it to me, I accept it, and I shall doubtless enjoy it. But rival *me*. I defy you."

Waden chuckled. "Come to the Residency when it pleases you. We'll drink together."

"You'll sit for me. I'll need both holographs and sketches. You'll come to my studio for the holographs, where I have the equipment."

"When?"

"Tomorrow at ten."

"You realize I have other schedules."

"At ten."

Waden laughed. "I accept. As for you, come when you please." He walked a distance, looked back. "Bring Keye to the Residency, if it suits."

"She may be amused. I wouldn't venture to predict."

Waden nodded, turned, walked his way back toward the Residency, as everyone walked in Kierkegaard, except the incapacitated, the infant, and the drivers of trucks which carried things too large or too heavy for carrying by hand. Herrin turned a cold eye on the apprentices, who put themselves as coldly to work, knowing they could not daunt him, but each attempting to assert an independent reality. They were not accustomed to such handling as he gave them . . . well, but they took it.

He walked about, directing this and that team as he had

previously. He found himself ill at ease, knowing the temper of Waden Jenks, knowing that Waden had touched perilously close to the heart of matters. Cade Jenks was dead, and this proved certain things about Waden which Herrin had suspected; but then, there had been in that father-son relationship no love, or pleasure, or respect.

He also had power, by reason of his position in the University and in Kierkegaard. The apprentices regarded *him* with fear, because he had authority to hire and dismiss any Student or laborer from the project. At a word from him even an Apprentice would be banished from University and disgraced, condemned to the provinces; or a worker sent among the invisible Unemployed. The Students coveted the chance at Jenks Square. The laborers coveted the government support. They worked with zeal, in consequence. The dread with which they regarded that possibility of dismissal and the pride they took in being assigned to the project were evident in their application.

He watched the stacks of stone arranged, which were already waist high, and eventually, toward dusk, he spoke to his chief apprentice, Leona Pace, and saw to it that due care would be taken in unloading the stone which was still coming in on trucks from the warehouses.

"I shall hold you accountable," he told her, "if any damage is done; and twice accountable if there is any weak stone set into the structure. Remember the weight this foundation must bear. If there is a flaw in any stone, however it came there, set it aside and hold it for my personal inspection. If you have doubt in any stone, set it aside. The supply of stone is endless; the State provides. Am I understood?"

"Master Law, without question."

He nodded, walked away, through the stone circles and to that apartment overlooking Jenks Square which belonged to Keye.

"I've been watching," she told him when he had, in front of the window looking down on the building, taken her in his arms and kissed her. Their relationship was by turns cool and by turns warm, and lately the latter.

"It looks like nothing at all as yet," he said, relieving her of any duty to flatter him. He let her lead him to the table. She had promised dinner, and dinner there was, with flower-lights drifting in bowls among the dishes, and incense in the air. Keye had a servant to provide such touches, while he had never bothered, tossing things aside when done with them, to live in a warren of discarded stones and clothes piled according to washed and unwashed, cleanly—he was obsessive about cleanliness—but he confined his art to stone, not house-holding.

This was not, however, to say that he failed to appreciate beauty offered him. He sat down, gave the flowerlight nearest a push which sent it drifting through the maze of the crystal serpentine bowl and smiled at her.

"That was Waden down there today."

"What, spying from the window? I thought you had classes."

"Canceled still. The official, dreary respect goes on. You've been my sole entertainment—watching the trucks, considering your plight."

"How, plight?"

"You understand me. Nothing escapes you; you take such pride in it."

"Because I work for him?"

"No."

"You mean to drag this through dessert, I can see."

"I trust not. I've warned you, but you see only endurance. You plan to outlast him, encompass him, and he . . . has his vanity. There was a time you knew where you were going; now you apply to Waden Jenks for a roadmap."

"I am not political."

"Where do you live?"

He frowned, patient with her games. "On Freedom, in Sartre, in Kierkegaard, in the University, in specific—how fine shall I dice it?"

"Until you smell the air and know you *are* political."

"I confess to it then, but I'm politically unconsenting. I live in larger scope than Waden Jenks; our arenas are different."

"Yours embraces his. As *you* embrace that monument—shells within shells—he won't laugh when he perceives that Reality."

"You are uncommonly keen this evening."

"Only talkative."

"He asked you to the Residency, as my companion."

"What, are *you* going?"

"I said yes."

"Well, I'll not. Those who become embraced by stones of another's shaping . . . take what shapes they dictate, don't they? I have my own comforts. I'll watch. Come *here*, when you will; I'll even give you the key. It may be a refuge more convenient than your own."

"I suspect you of unguessed talents. You think I've erred."

"Go if you like."

He smiled slowly. "I shall, and come, and take the key too. I thank you."

"I remind you I am fastidious in housekeeping."

There was a time when he looked into Keye's eyes and saw something reserved, and again not; he was never sure. Keye deserved regard. He had never caught her at humor, but sometimes, he suspected, at kindness. When he was with her sometimes he smelled earth and old boards, recalled a world quite different from the competition of the University and the fierce, cold Residency. Recalled that provincial reality where in their Self and for their pleasure, or perhaps because they were bound by primal instincts—his parents had surprised him with kind acts. He had treasured surprises of that nature, unpredictable in the main because there was no particular reason for them, and they were small—a favorite dish, something of the sort. Keye, he thought, had come from such a provincial origin, even farther up the river; Keye did some things which had nothing to do with the study and practice of creative ethics, simply because there were unrecognized patterns within her behavior.

Or doing such things pleased her, because the following of childhood patterns was in itself satisfying, and she played purposeful games watching others' reactions to them, which was within *her* art. Keye's field was, like his and unlike Waden's, creative, and at moments when he thought of that, he reckoned Keye as greater than Waden gave her credit for being.

"No," he said suddenly. "I'll not take the key. And you know my reasoning."

"What, you surrender to Waden's bending but not to mine?"

"I have wandered between both. My eyes are open."

"Pursue your liberty."

She mocked him now. "Waden has erred about you," he said. "Go to the Residency. Exert your influence there."

"At your suggestion? Or at Waden's either?" She lowered her lids like a curtain and looked up again smiling. "I am the only *free* individual in Kierkegaard. Go or stay. I am immovable from my Self. I'm the ethicist, and I am continually creating the ethic in my personal reality, which I am doing at this moment. Consider all my advice to you in that light."

He thought it humor for a moment. Then he knew otherwise. He rose, stared down at her in outrage and distress. She continued to smile. "There is a reason," he said, recovering his mental balance, "that you tell me this."

"I refuse comment, perhaps . . . but I don't give reasons. Part of my creativity lies in letting others shape themselves around their own guesswork. You are—what? Omnipotent? Waden's servant? Mine?"

For a second moment she had thrown him totally off his balance, and then he smiled and nodded. Let Keye think as she would. "Good evening," he said. "I prefer a little quietude this evening, and I think we're approaching one of our cooler periods. When you've resolved your personal dilemmas, or when you find it convenient . . . I'll hear you, but I'm tired this evening, Keye, indeed I am. First Waden, and then Waden again tomorrow. So if this is your humor, do without me."

"You exude destruction. Perhaps I want you clear of me."

"Power never comes from retreat, Keye."

She stared at him, wise and amused as Keye could look, perhaps agreeing, perhaps refuting him by her very silence. He sighed, denied all but a good dinner, and walked out the familiar door, down the clean pebblestone hall, the same as every other hall in Kierkegaard, and down the stairs which was like every other stairs, all a blank slate which waited this generation, and his talent, and students of his teaching.

I shall be here, he thought, after them all. It's my nature to take in inspiration, and upon that thought, he suffered such a narrowing of the heart, such an apprehension that he stopped in his tracks there in the stairwell and leaned against the pebbled wall, thinking a moment and cold with fright. An art which was necessarily dependent on inspiration arriving from external forces was—perhaps enslaved to those forces; and if it was, then he was. Keye could be right. It shook the assumption of a lifetime and demanded thinking.

He wandered out then, through the foyer and onto the

street where the white electric glare lit small black figures against the white stone and the cranes wheezed and lifted their burdens like grotesque giants. He saw yet another course of stone going into place as a view which had been open in Kierkegaard all the years of his residence here became forever obstructed, imprisoned, cut off.

He built a snare for the eye; he did things until now unthought of; he discovered unconsidered and unfelt dimensions to his own work which verged on the chaotic.

An irrational force, a madness, a dark and Dionysian force. That was his work, which begun, acquired its own momentum, which seized minds and impressed them with its own Reality.

Kierkegaard changed. It was begun. Keye and Waden had no power against it.

He laughed as he had laughed the sunny day he stood on that bronze circle marking the center of Kierkegaard and spun; but no one would ever stand there again, no foot in all of time to come would likely tread that spot, no one ever have that vantage which had inspired the work. Even if ten thousand years made a crumbled heap of all man had done on the site of Kierkegaard, a hill would stand there, of crumbled marble, of ruin, and memories. A city would have stood there, the heart of which was forever sucked in and warped and changed by his mind. The world would not be the same, since that heap of stone began to stand there, and never could be what it would have been had there been no Herrin Law.

But Waden Jenks had permitted the work, urged it.

The perplexities overcame him. He had interrupted the workers with his laughter, and now with his silence. They stood there, surely wondering who was there in the shadows. But then they began work again, no one investigating. There were madmen in Kierkegaard, the invisibles, who sometimes with sound or action intruded on the Reality of the city—who screamed, sometimes, or laughed, as if they made some attempt to be seen by the sane. Herrin drew breath, and walked quietly away from Keye's apartment building, and through the peripheries of the work.

"Sir," apprentices murmured, recognizing him now, and offering him respect. He walked on, paying no attention to them, casting instead a critical eye to the stone which gleamed white in the darkness, sheened with the artifical lamps. No flaws were evident.

"Sir," said Leona Pace, who came to intercept him. "I thought you'd gone."

"Going," he said equably, and walked on.

He refused to be disturbed. The physical fact of the sculpture reassured him that all Keye's hopes to manipulate him and all Waden's confidence that he did so . . . were the necessary illusions of Keye Lynn and Waden Jenks. *This*, this stone, was real. He was not deluded into believing the substance was real; he discounted that. The *shaping* far more than the substance of the stone . . . that was the reality. And the shaping was his.

He walked . . . up the long extent of Main, through the narrow archway in the firebush hedge, onto Port Street, intending to go to the studio in the University, to apply his restlessness to his labors . . . but the Residency was before him and he stopped, stared up at the bleak pebblestone façade which was identical to that of the University, or a warehouse, or anything else.

This too, I shall change, he thought, conceiving further ambitions, wondering which was the more important, to involve himself immediately in the Residency alterations or to intervene in the proposed new hemisphere programs.

MAN, said the plaque inset above the Residency entry, is THE MEASURE OF ALL THINGS.

And he smiled, knowing how that was set forth to the masses of Freedom, and what the real truth was, for in University they taught another maxim: The strongest survives, the weaker serve, the weakest perish.

Who am I? the masses in the provincial schools were taught to ask.

The masses went on asking, diverted by the question and never really wanting the answer if they had known it. The sign was for them. They took pride in it. They saw the world in their own measure.

The Students at University learned a second question. *What is reality?* They doubted all previous questions.

And a very few attained to the Last Statement.

I.

He smiled somewhat cruelly at the sign, which to the masses promised control of their destinies.

Perhaps the mad, he thought, *have seen their conditions.* Inferiority was a bitter mouthful. The mad in Kierkegaard were one step ahead of the sane and subservient . . . because most of those out there limited their thoughts—lest they see what the mad had seen, that they were not in control of anything.

Must not think further—or go mad, lacking power, which, after all, makes life worth living.

And is there one, he wondered (the inevitable question), only one man, after all, for whom the whole species exists? But humanity had no existence, of course, save in the mind of the one man who warped all that was about himself.

Himself.

He was, after all, very comfortable this night. He had simply recovered his previous state, before Keye, which was solitude. He thought of the first night he had begun to realize his solitude, the first night he had begun to conceive of himself as *psychurgos* and not as child, the night the visitor had come to tell him he was different.

His parents. Perrin. In fact his thoughts had not tended that way twice in a day in a very long time. He would bring them to Kierkegaard when his great work was finished. They would be an excellent test of it. The anticipation of the effect on them excited him.

Accomplishment, he thought, did not diminish goals: it opened new ones. To reach back to Camus and to alter that place too . . . one of his apprentices, trained by the work here, would suffice to change Camus. And to change his parents' and sister's lives, by enveloping them in his influence, giving them prominence in Camus. . . .

He smiled, self-pleased, confident, and walked from the facade of the Residency and its power and its philosophy toward his own domain at the University. He never meant to let Waden come too close to him, as Keye had come, until she tried to maneuver him and discovered that she could not.

He whistled, walking along the walk beneath the streetlamps, disturbing the night because it was his to disturb.

A shadow confronted him, gangling, robed. He *saw* it because it startled him, coming out of that patch of shadow between the two buildings. Or perhaps it had been there all along and he had not perceived it. He had truly not seen one of the Others in—he had forgotten how long. He had learned how not to see them, out of politeness.

It stood there, a blob of midnight in the light of the street-lamp, and from within the hood seemed to stare at him, a question posed. His path was blocked. The ahnit made himself . . . itself? inconvenient to his progress.

He walked round it and curiously—for he was beyond such curiosity—he had a nagging impulse to look back, to see if it regarded his departing back, or if he should see it taking its own way.

Anathema.

It did not exist. He refused it existence. An inevitable question occurred to him, regarding his existence in its eyes.

His mind rebounded perversely to his analysis of the insane, who confronted a reality which swallowed them, and who thereafter, had to ignore all realities, or establish their own rules.

He laughed nervously, silently, because the night was no longer empty of threat to him. He went not to his studio, but to the Fellows' Hall in the University, and sat at that table which he and Waden had shared on a certain night, familiar scarred wood.

The University was created for Waden, and created Herrin Law, sculptor.

He drank his beer and sat alone, because he was a Master and there were no younger Students who dared approach or question him; because he was known to be powerful and most of good sense would not come to him uninvited, fearing the edge of his wit. His apprentices had spread his reputation of late and the self-knowing retreated from hazard.

He was alone. Solitary in his Universe, the only real point.

X

Master Herrin Law: Does emotion originate from within or without your reality?
Apprentice: Within. There are no external events.

> *Master Law: Is the stimulus to emotion also internal?*
> *Apprentice: Sir, no external events exist.*
> *Master Law: Am I within your reality?*
> *Apprentice: (Silence).*
> *Master Law: That is a correct answer.*

Waden Jenks tolerated the sitting, suffered in silence, because to admit discomfort and then go on to bear it was to admit he was constrained. Herrin prolonged the misery in self-contained humor, took whatever shots might be minutely necessary, sketched from several angles, after resetting the lighting with meticulous care.

And Waden, perched on his uncushioned chair, sat rigidly obedient.

"The lighting," Herrin said, "will be from a number of sources. I take the seasons into account; apprentices are running the matter in the computer, so that the lighting will be exact from season to season, the sun hovering hour by hour in a series of what appear to be design-based apertures. The play of—"

"Spare me. I'll see the finished effect. I trust your talent."

Herrin smiled, undisturbed. Darkened an area beneath the chin and smiled the more.

"A little haste," said Waden. "I have appointments."

"Ah?"

"A ship in orbit. An ordinary thing."

"Ah."

"There is some hazard. This is McWilliams's *Singularity*."

Herrin lifted an eyebrow, nonplused.

"An irregular client, one of the more troublesome. I'd like you to be there, Artist."

Both eyebrows. "Me? Where, at the port?"

"The Residency, my friend."

"What, you want sketches?"

Waden smiled. "I find the opinion of the second mind of Freedom—an asset. You have an insight into character. I value your assessment. Observe the man and tell me what you'd surmise about him."

"Interesting. An interesting proposal. I bypass your naïve assumption. I'll come."

"Of course you will."

He stopped in midshadow, made it a reflective pause, studiously ignoring Waden, refusing at this moment to interpret him.

XI

Apprentice: Master Law, what is the function of Art in the State?

Master Law: The question holds an incorrect assumption.

Apprentice: What assumption, sir?

Master Law: That Art is in the State.

And on the morrow the shuttle was down and Camden McWilliams was in the Residency.

Herrin wore Student's Black; it was stark and sufficiently dramatic for confrontations. He sat in the corner of Waden's office, refusing to be amazed at the splendor of the decoration, much of the best of the University culled for the private ownership of the First Citizen. He knew the individual styles: the desk with the carved legs, definitely Genovese; the delicate chair which bore Waden's healthy weight, Martin's; the paintings, Disa Welby; the very rugs on the floor, work of Zad Pirela, meant as wall hangings, and here trod upon as carpet.

He was offended. Vastly offended. He observed, catalogued, refused to react. It was Waden's prerogative to treat such things with casual abuse, since Waden had the power to do so; he recovered his humor and smiled to himself, thinking that there was one work Waden could not swallow, but which engulfed him.

Meanwhile he sketched, idly, and looked up with cool disinterest when functionaries showed in captain Camden McWilliams.

A black man of outlandish dress, bright colors, a big man

who assumed the space about him and who had probably given the functionaries difficulty. Waden greeted McWilliams coldly, and Herrin simply smiled and flipped the page of his sketchbook to begin again.

"McWilliams of the irregular merchanter *Singularity*," Waden Jenks said, failing to hold out his hand. "Herrin Law, Master of Arts."

"McWilliams," Herrin said cooly.

McWilliams took him in with a glance and frowned at Waden. "Wanted to see," he began without preamble, "what kind of authority we have here. You're old Jenks's son, are you?"

"You've been informed," Waden said. "Come the rest of the way to your point, McWilliams of *Singularity*."

"Just looking you over." McWilliams studiously spat on the Pirela carpet. "Figure the same policies apply."

"I follow old policies where pleasant and convenient to me. That I see you at all is more remarkable than you know, for reasons that you won't understand. Outsiders don't. You'll accept the same goods at the same rate and we'll accept no nonsense. Trade here is not necessary."

"We," said McWilliams, "have the ability to level this city."

"Good. I trust you also have the ability to harvest grain and to wait about while the new crop grows. Perhaps the military will assist with the next harvest."

McWilliams chuckled softly and spat a second time. "Good enough, Jenks. Go on about your business. We're loading at port. You know my face now and I know yours."

"Sufficient exchange, McWilliams."

"What's this—thing—in the city?"

"Thing, McWilliams?"

"This thing in the middle of town. Scan doesn't lie. What are you doing out there?"

"Art. A decorative program."

McWilliams's eyes rested coldly on him. "Nothing military, would it be?"

"Nothing military." For once Waden Jenks looked mildly surprised. "Take the tour, McWilliams. There's no restriction in Kierkegaard. Wander our streets as you will."

"*This* city? Hell, sooner."

"The driver will take you to the port." Waden made a

temple of his hands and smiled past them. "A safe trip, McWilliams."

"Huh," McWilliams said, and turned and walked out.

Herrin filled in a line, shadowed an ear, languidly looked up into Waden's waiting eyes. "Barbarian," he judged. "Limited in formal debate but abundantly intelligent. *Can* he level the city?"

"Undoubtedly."

Herrin's insouciance failed him. For a moment he almost credited Waden with humor at his expense, and then revised his opinion.

"Freedom," said Waden Jenks, "navigates a black and perilous sea, Herrin. And *I* guide it. And I see the directions of it. And I shape things beyond this city, beyond Sartre, beyond Freedom itself. I am a power in wider affairs, and when they come calling . . . I deal with them. This much you should see, when you portray *me*, Herrin Law."

For a moment Herrin was taken aback. "My art will encompass you," he said. "And comprehend you in all senses of the word. The man saw my work, did he not? From that great height, he saw it."

"That pleases you."

"It's an intriguing thought."

"Their vision is considerably augmented to be able to do it. Kierkegaard is a very small city, by what I know."

"We are at our beginning."

"Indeed. So am I. Freedom is my beginning, not my limit."

"We once talked of hubris."

"And discounted it. Shape your stones, Artist. My way is scope. We talked about that too. You'll never see the posterity you work toward. You'll only hope it exists . . . someday. But I'll see the breadth I aim for."

"But not the duration."

The words came from his mouth unchecked, unthought, uncautious. For a moment Waden's smile looked deathly, and a very real fear came into his eyes.

"You serve my interests. Go on. Pursue your logic."

"You'll carry my reputation with yours." Herrin followed the argument like a beast to the kill, savoring the moment, hating the role in which perpetual caution had cast him with this man. "Mutual advantage."

Waden smiled. That was always a good answer. It was effective, because he had then to wonder if Waden conceived of an answer. It was possible that Waden did; his wit was not easily overcome.

And Herrin smiled, because it was a good answer for him to return.

So henceforth alone, he thought firmly. *Each to his own interests.* He was linked to Waden in one way and severed from him irrevocably in another, because the war was in the open.

"You've seen," Waden said, "all that could interest you. I won't keep you from your important work."

Herrin slowly completed a line, shaded one, sealing the image of the foreigner in all his dark force. Flipped the notebook shut and rose, left without even an acknowledgment that there was anyone else in the room but himself.

Creative ethics, Keye called it.

But in fact the visit did shake him; and when he walked out under the sky, leaving the Residency, he could not but think of a vast machine orbiting over their heads, observing what passed in Kierkegaard from an unassailable height . . . that there was a force above them which had a certain power over their existence.

He did not look up, because of course there was nothing of it to be seen; and he shrugged off the feeling of it. Laughed softly, at the thought that Freedom ignored outside forces as they ignored the invisibles; that in effect he had just spent a time talking to an invisible.

The man had spat on the Pirela weavings, had spat to contemn Waden Jenks and all Freedom, and Waden had treated that affront as invisible too, but it did not remove the spittle from the priceless artwork.

That man, the thought kept insinuating itself into his peace of mind, that man despised the greatest political power on Freedom, and the work of one of Freedom's great artists, and walked out, because there had been nothing to do.

Waden Jenks might have had him killed on the spot. Might have, potentially. But that ship was still up there with the power to level Freedom. Camden McWilliams had refused the rare chance for a closer sight of Kierkegaard, from fear? from distrust? . . . or further contempt?

He refused to think more on such matters. The man was an invisible. Meditating on invisibles was unproductive. Invisibles had nothing to do with reality, having rejected their own.

The anology was incomplete: the ship and Camden McWilliams possessed power.

Herrin shivered in the daylight and walked on the way that the outsider had rejected, into the town.

The work progressed. He reached the Square, where the eighth course of stone was being moved into place, and even while that work progressed, apprentices were at work on the lowermost courses, some mapping the places to cut, some actually cutting with rapid precision, so that already the three shells, the touchpoints of the interior curtain-walls, and the foot of the central support, showed some indication of shaping, troughs, folds, incisions.

A further portion of the view which had existed on this site since the initial layout of Kierkegaard—was gone. He refused to look up toward Keye's apartment. She might be there, might be at the University. She would spend her evenings at least contemplating what went on below. The noise would intrude on her sleep, impossible for her to ignore. He wondered how she reasoned with that.

He walked round the structure, actually inside it with a palpable feeling of enclosure. The art of it began. Other walkers, ordinary citizens, had ventured into it cautiously, because it sat in the main intersection of Kierkegaard. They gawked about them in spite of their personal dignity, avoiding the ominous machinery, touching the stone in furtive curiosity. This *satisfied* him. He found himself immensely excited when he watched a stray child, more outward than her elders, stand with mouth open and then run the patterns of the curving walls until a stern parent collected her.

And for the second time, he saw one of the Others.

The workers saw nothing, nor did the walkers, who continued without attention to it, perfectly in command of their realities at least as regarded invisibles.

But Herrin saw it, midnight-robed, walking through the structure, lingering to examine it as the child had, walking the patterns.

And that did not satisfy him. He turned from the sight, trying to pretend to others that he had noticed nothing, and perhaps their own concentration on their own reality was so

intense that they could not notice his action in connection
with the apparition.

Suddenly he suffered a further vision. Having seen the one
midnight robe, he saw others on the outskirts, standing there,
outside one of the half-built gateways. Three figures. He was
not aware whether he noticed them now because he had seen
the one and the shock of the night encounter was still powerful, or perhaps it was in fact the Work which drew them, and
they had never been there before.

He wiped them from his mind, turned to his own work,
which was the central column. Leona Pace was not at hand,
presumably being off about some important business. He interrupted an apprentice to look at diagrams, found everything
in order, bestowed no compliments. They were not expected
to exercise their own inspirations, but to execute his, and they
were all doing so with absolute precision: had any failed, that
one would have been discharged with prejudice. He pushed
the apprentice aside, made a minor change, sketching with
black on the stone itself, and the apprentice obediently al-
tered the computer-generated sheet which was the master
plan.

So doing, he put himself back to work and put the external
from his mind. He worked until suppertime, and involuntarily
thought of Keye, looked from the incomplete hemisphere of
the dome, and saw the warmth of her window light in the
dusk. He recalled sweet scents and a meticulous order, and
the servant's excellent taste, and suffered a spasm of regret
for their continued separation. His mind flashed back to
Law's Valley, and to other such warm comforts, now lost. He
prepared to make his solitary way back to University, and
left the work in the capable charge of Leona Pace, who had
returned from the shipping terminal and her own selection of
the stone, a zeal he silently approved. Pace looked shadowed,
hungry, exhausted; she kept at the work nonetheless, for her
reasons, probably having to do with insecurity in her subordi-
nates. He did not blame her: Pace was extraordinary, and
anyone of lesser ability had to be a frustration and a worry
to her.

He valued Pace, might have made closer acquaintance with
her, with the thought of filling some of that solitude; there
were looks he received from her which hinted a desire for his
approval, which might lead to dependency on it, which might

in turn lead to a relationship different and more controllable than he had known.

But no, experience of Keye and Waden argued caution was in order. Pace was zealous. Ambitious. He was at the moment too weary to deal with someone of ability and possible labyrinthine motive. Such entanglements with apprentices were all potential hazard.

Dinner, he told himself, at the Fellows' Hall; he still wore his black, and he would be inconspicuous as Herrin Law could ever be. A solitary dinner. Solitary tea. Solitary bed.

XII

Master Keye Lynn: How do the realities of Freedom coexist?

Master Law: They don't.

Master Lynn: How do you reconcile the realities of Freedom?

Master Law: I don't.

Master Lynn: How are lower degrees of intelligence able to maintain their separate realities?

Master Law: They delude themselves; they're part of mine.

He departed the structure, where lights had come on, glaring with their nightly brilliance, and walked along an increasingly deserted street past the ever-same buildings, taking no thought for his safety.

The slight traffic of Main vanished entirely at the hedge of Port Street. He passed through the arch of the firebushes, and experienced ever so slight a fear, outraged by it as soon as he had come out again into the deepening dusk of the street, out in front of the Residency, in which rows of lights showed interior life. He was not accustomed to fear. He was the most confident of men; had every reason for confidence. Suddenly he took on caution in harmless streets, as if there were something there which nagged at his attention, an eroding of safety, a thing which appeared only in the corner of the eye, as the blanking color of the Others and the invisibles had screened them from eyes which had learned not to see that color and that robed shape. He had never been so troubled, had never had such sick fantasies.

He was an Artist, and *saw* details which others could not see. That was his art.

And did he then, in his skill, begin to lose that ability which screened out madness and the irrational?

I, he insisted to himself, and looked to the Residency façade.

MAN IS THE MEASURE OF ALL THINGS. MAN. MAN . . . and nothing else.

I.

There was a rumbling. Shuttles had come and gone at the port many times in his life in Kierkegaard; no one heard them or deigned to pay them notice, except those whose business it was to deal with the fact. But in the dark, and the slight chill, the disturbance of the air could not be ignored. The thunderclouds gathered like a summer storm, and he lifted his eyes to the far end of Port Street, where a light rose in the sky. And because he was alone and had no shielding distraction he found himself looking up, and up, and up, following the moving light of the shuttle, against a sky utterly black near the glare of the port lights, and then sprinkled with stars as the light climbed higher.

He was not wont to look up at all. He knew vaguely that the stars were suns like their own and that such suns had planets like their own and that organization drew those worlds together into complexities of politics. Knew that there were renegade powers, like Camden McWilliams. But for the first time he saw how *many* stars there were.

It was like looking down from a height, realizing that number. For a moment his balance deserted him. The *I* became less than it had been, a reality valid on Freedom, in Freedom's context.

Scope. Waden's art reached for those points of light. His art—bound to Waden—would go out there. Waden called himself Apollonian, orderly, light-loving and logical, but what he perceived in that scattering of dust was disquietingly Dionysian, chaotic, dark, and random.

Why do they stay in order? he wondered of the stars; and recalled half-heard tapes of natural structure, and forces, and his own art, which had to do with the architecture of a dome, and of inner, chemical structures of stone, vision plummeting from macroscopic to microscopic in one dizzying contraction and out again. He realized that he was staring, that someone might see him and think him gone mad, but he had never been concerned for the opinions of lesser minds; had disturbed Jenks Square with equanimity, uncaring. Now he felt exposed, catching a glimpse of something, like the Others, which refused to fit.

I, he reminded himself, defying the stars, and lowered his eyes to the street and walked across it.

Why? The question echoed in his mind, unwelcome; along with *how far?* and *how wide?* and *how old?*

I.

The invisibles looked at Reality and flinched from it, retreating into madness. His art was to see, and to go on seeing. It occurred to him that something dangerous was happening, that he had started a chain of events which led precipitately somewhere, and there was no stopping it.

He heard Waden asserting an exterior reality as valid. The University had been founded for Waden.

And might not other things have served Waden Jenks?

If he were sane, he thought, he would back off from such questions, which kept demanding others and others until the perspectives went spiraling up and down from molecule to star and back again.

He kept walking, past the safe front of the University, ignoring the hunger which he had nursed past a neglected lunch, the faint savor of food in the air from all the houses in Kierkegaard. He followed the avenue, which was deserted, and came closer and closer to the port.

Fear was there. He knew that it was. Fear was what he pursued. He walked as far as the open gate in the wire fence which ran the circumference of the port area—fenced for what reason was not clear, for there were no guards, no one defending the access. There were lights, glaring in the night like the lights which he could see if he looked back, where the glow of the work in Jenks Square lit the darkness above the hedges and the tops of buildings. Lights glared in the area from which the shuttle itself might have lifted, a bare circle of machinery lit with floodlamps all up and down its ugly and yet interesting height, like the cranes which labored to place the stone in Jenks Square.

And figures, robed, walked among booths garishly draped under the fieldside floods. He stared, recognizing them as Others, or invisibles, there for trade.

He knew that invisibles somehow pilfered by night in the port market, where citizens of Kierkegaard traded by day, disdaining any robed intruders out of their time, but there was no mention that *this* went on by night, organized, booths manned—if they *were* men—money changing hands from opened cashboxes. . . .

He walked farther, facing fear, because it was there, as he would have faced down Waden or Keye or anyone else fit to rival him. Fear ran the aisles, skipped along almost visibly in the rippling shadows of robes which should have been invisible to his trained perceptions; but it was night, and robes cast shadows, and shadows were everywhere. There was no one like himself, a citizen. Pilfered goods disappeared and no one cared to complain, because had the invisibles been a problem, something would have been done about it, the solution so often proposed and never, because they did not care for the untidiness, carried out.

To kill them all, some had argued in University, would remove a blight. And whoever proposed the solution stood self-consciously admitting that they existed.

And who knows how many there are? another had proposed. Or how we should track them all? They do no harm.

In point of fact, no one knew . . . how many there were, who had gone mad. No one knew how many ahnit there were, or how many robes here might conceal one or the other. The invisibles had stopped being human.

Perhaps they bred, making more invisibles. If so they were quiet about it, and perhaps the offspring, lacking proper care, died; no one asked. No one noticed. It was not good health to take overmuch thought in the matter.

As for ahnit, they were not even in basic question. They were a separate rationality. *The proper study of man is man,* the maxim ran.

Who had proposed such a thing, when their ancestors had

been merchants, or at least merchants had been among their ancestors? Who had made the decisions, when they found this perfect world that was Freedom and laid down the Reality which existed here? A Jenks?

But once . . . all their ancestors had been up, out there, far away.

Once. . . .

He cancelled that reality, preferring to start time over again. It was his Reality, his option. He smiled self-confidently, walked up to a booth manned by an invisible and found the meat pastry there attractive. He gathered up two of the hot pies, not seeing the invisible who sat there watching him, and humorously walked away, eating the invisible pie and quite pleased with the taste of it. Men could pilfer under the same law as invisibles. No one was going to ask him for payment. No one dared, because they did not want to be noticed.

Much more savory than what was served in the Fellows' Hall. He recalled an old saying about stolen fruit and, finishing one pie, sought a beer amongst the booths.

Quite a different reality, he thought, intrigued now that the disturbance of the day had been settled—food was what he had evidently needed to settle his stomach and his metaphysics. He was fascinated by the swirl of no-color and no-substance against the powerful glare of the port lights where the shuttle had gone back to the invisible ship and its invisible threat. Quite, quite fascinating, this walk through an invisible's dream of reality, where madmen went about commerce and no-men stalked about on their own inscrutable business.

There must be a certain economy to allow it to function. Sane farmers grew crops, which invisibles pilfered, which in turn *he* pilfered, and it all somehow balanced, because what was pilfered was sold, turnabout day and night, and his small consumption merely fed the engine that was Kierkegaard and Sartre itself, which fed this mass as well as the daylight trade.

And how did the ahnit fit in? Some of the goods in the booths—the clothes—the robes which ahnit and men wore . . . ahnit robes. Ahnit Jewelry. He paused and *took* a piece, turned it in his hand, found it, with its convolute patterns, of passing skill. He pinned it to his collar, laughing at the conceit. An economy which functioned on universal theft,

with sales only among like and like; founded on the principle
that no one stole, just pilfered. He walked on, saw one of the
University stamped hammers for sale, doubtless pilfered from
Jenks Square, from *his* work. Amazing. He declined to repos-
sess it. It was a minor item and heavy to be carrying about.
Let them have it.

He found his drink in a brightly draped booth which
passed out an assortment of mugs. He appropriated what was
destined for another hand, right from under the invisible's
reach, and walked his way, consuming his second pie, tasting
cool beer and dazzled by amazements right and left.

When he had done he set the mug down, reckoning it
would be pilfered back along the circuitous route, likely back
to the very same booth from which he had taken it. *Nothing*
could get lost in the labyrinthine system. He had lived within
it all his life and had never quite seen it so clearly delineated,
so vividly exercised . . . for even in Law's Valley things had
vanished, to turn up again in market in Camus, and it was
not good form to question.

Kill the invisibles? He wondered. How would civilization
survive if not for them? Where would be the humor in that?

Not to go searching the market for a lost plowshare? Not
to have the confidence it would turn up again? No one ever
hungered because of it. And a good many times were never
missed, or were missed with gratitude, and discovered by another with pleasure, whenever some citizen bought it back
again. This was somewhat like the country markets, indeed it
was, and the few new-goods warehouses in town were dull by
comparison. Only in Camus there had been just the Place,
where goods tended to appear, and remain, and perhaps—he
had never wondered—there was also this nighttime activity.

By day, simple citizens; by night, invisibles. The same mer-
chandise.

A balance, indeed.

He had quite shed his fear and walked now in utter aban-
don.

An ahnit set itself in his path, and from within the hood a
glitter of eyes regarded him with such directness that he forgot himself, and stopped, and then had to recover his self-
possession and walk around the obstacle, instead of
employing that graceful sidestep one used when the obstacle
was expected. He was shaken. It was deliberate. It was very

near aggression. The thought occurred to him that if a citizen should ever be found dead in Kierkegaard—and it happened—the inquiry did not extend beyond citizens and natural causes.

He kept going in his chosen path, which took him again to the gate, and to Port Street.

He looked back. For the first time in his adult life he committed such an indiscretion, and there was an ahnit there.

A shadow, a robed shadow on the street, beneath the lights by the gate. It had followed.

He had looked—and never meant to again—but this one time he had looked, simply to prove himself wrong. His apprehension had been correct, and thereafter, alone or in public, whenever beset with the temptation to yield to the urge to look behind him, whenever insecure in his own reality he would remember . . . once . . . there had been something there. He shivered. He hurried.

The University doors received him, solid wood, carved, safe and sturdy. They closed behind him and he walked down the corridors toward Fellows' Hall, hearing the slight boisterousness from it long before he reached it. He sought the familiar, the banal, desperately.

XIII

Student: Master Law, is friendship possible?

Master Law: What is friendship?

Second Student: We propose it's a sharing of realities.

Master Law: Do you also propose to step into the same river in the same instant and in the same place?

Student: Perhaps . . . friendship is equivalency of realities.

Master Law: How do you establish that equivalency?

Student: If we were equal.

Master Law: In all respects?

*Student: In the important ones. In the ones we consider
   important. Is that possible, sir?*
Master Law: Have you not equally defined rivalry?
Second Student: If we agreed.
*Master Law: If common reality is your reality, it exists,
   within that referent. If either of you exists, which is
   by no means certain.*

He betook himself to bed in the studio, having a cot there
for occasions of late work; it was his own familiar clutter and
he had had a great many beers. He reckoned that the best
cure for his troubles.

Overwork. He had overstrained himself, and his agitated
brain was seeking occupation even when it reasonably had
none, simply burning off adrenalin; that was the source of his
bizarre fancies.

But when he sat on his cot and reviewed the sketches he
had made in his sketchbook, he stopped on the last one he
had done of Waden, knowing that another turn of the page
was going to bring the nightmare back again.

He turned it, because he could not refrain. The image of
Camden McWilliams was there, black and broad-shouldered
and solid, refuting invisibility. He had sketched an invisible,
and brought it home with him. And on his collar was another
thing, which he had forgotten, until he saw the outsider
again.

He pulled off the ahnit brooch and it lay chill in his palm.
He was numbed by his evening's drinking. He sat there un-
sure what he ought to do with the thing, which was . . . fine.
It was no-color, lapis, nothing very precious, but . . . fine.
There was no destroying such a thing. It went against all his
sensibilities.

He laid it atop the portrait of Camden McWilliams, who
had spat on priceless art, canceling him from his thoughts.
He lay down on his cot, with the light on, and stared about
him at what had been real and solid and true for so many
years, and finally the Reality reasserted itself. *He* reasserted
it, and snugged into the warmth and slept a drunken sleep.

His head hurt in the morning, as expected; he had a bewildered recollection of himself and his wanderings, and with
light pouring in the studio window and peace everywhere the

series of encounters seemed entirely surreal and his fear
somewhat amusing.

He shaved, washed, dressed, in spirits as ebullient as an
aching head and slight embarrassment would allow.

Keye, he decided. The fact was that he missed Keye and
therefore he indulged himself in such nonsense. If he had had
Keye's apartment to go to he should never have been doing
such incredible things—the market, the *port* market at night,
of all things!—and making a spectacle of himself. He had
fallen quite seriously. He had let Keye disturb him, that was
it; she had gotten to him and he had wobbled from the blow.
There was nothing for it but to reestablish himself with her,
move back in on his own terms, ignore her attempts to
manipulate him. It could only make him stronger. He had to
school himself to withstand her undermining effects, and on
the contrary to affect her. He was the superior, and anything
else was unthinkable.

He dressed, and clipped the ahnit brooch to his collar,
which no citizen of Kierkegaard would *dare* do, adorning
himself with invisible jewelry made by invisibles and Others.
It smacked of madness.

But so did dancing in the main square of Kierkegaard, and
he had done that. And laughed there. And as for dread of
what others might *think*, he was too powerful for that. If they
thought they saw him wearing something which invisibles had
made, then let them say so; it was a dilemma for them, a discomfort for all about him, a challenge. He wanted challenges
this morning; he was, perhaps because of the headache, in an
aggressive mood, and the humor of it vastly appealed to him.

He swung out the door of his studio, headed for the
square, with a lightness in his step, skipping down the stairs.

He had met all there was to fear; had bested it; had come
out of a bad dream, and headed for his work with enthusi-
asm.

XIV

Waden Jenks: Ah, Herrin, respect me.
Master Law: Fear me, if I'm your outlet to the world.
Your substance flows through my hands.
Waden Jenks: I've told you what I fear. What do you
fear, Artist?

"I'm back," he announced that evening at Keye's door.
The servant let him in and Keye herself, about to sit down to
a solitary supper, betrayed herself with a slight lifting of the
brows.

"Oh. Should I be happy?"

"Be what you choose. I trust there's something in the pan-
try."

"See to it," Keye told the servant, waving her hand, and
indicated the other chair. "So you're back. And how much
else do you assume?"

"Oh, be yourself. I'd never interfere."

She dropped the smile, sat there looking as if something
had gone down the wrong way, and stared at him a moment.
He kept smiling, because if she threw him out he would have
won, and if she let him stay he would have won.

He stayed.

If Keye noticed the brooch she said nothing, nor touched
it, nor commented on the rift which had been between them.
Keye was either on the retreat or, falsely self-assured, thought
that she had won. He did not think the latter. "Have you,"
she asked, "moved to the Residency yet?"

He shrugged. "I'm waiting a moment of convenience. I've
been too busy lately to consider an interruption."

"The work out there is going much faster than I would
have believed."

"What, do I surprise you?"

54

"If you like."

"I'm satisfied with it."

He wondered for a moment about Keye. Meekness was not her style, but possibly she was lonely, as he was. He admitted that much, having also admitted to himself that he could live in solitude if he chose. And Keye, who was superior to all but him and Waden, had to have come to similar decisions.

His reality, he concluded, was flexible enough to tolerate Keye. And to laugh at her pretensions.

XV

Master Law: How fine shall I dice it?

Master Lynn: Until you smell the air and know you are political.

Master Law: I confess to it then; but I'm politically unconsenting. I live in large scope than Waden Jenks; our arenas are different.

Master Lynn: Yours embraces his. As you embrace that monument, shells within shells. He won't laugh when he perceives that Reality.

He looked out Keye's window at a night somewhat removed from that night, when the whole apartment was dark and the only light was coming in from the glaring floods outside. The noise went on, the grinding of cranes, the voices of workmen and the voices of apprentices giving orders, the occasional ring of hammer and chisel. The twelfth course was laid. What had been three rings from above, with the thick central pillar and the apparent random placement of additional touch-points to act as supports . . . began to show other curves. The inward curve of the dome began to be apparent, and the curve of the pillar which was headed to meet it in three levels. That slamming of pipe . . . the scaffolding was going into place, the supports which would hold the developing dome until the last courses could be laid, and their keystones settled. During the next several days, the cranes would work nonstop. The whole shell would be put up; lighting was being arranged interior to the shell as well as exterior. Apprentices with their computer printouts and their cutters would sit at the base of a surface completing their tasks in sculpture, while cranes swung the vast stones into place above them. The major perforations would be made only when the whole structure stood solid. Minor texturing proceeded.

He put on his clothes, disturbing Keye as little as possible: "Difficulty?" she lifted her head from the pillow to ask. "Restless," he said. "Make love?" she murmured politely. "No need," he said, and Keye snuggled contentedly into the sheets and pillows, having had what she wanted and as happy, he knew well enough, to have the bed to herself thereafter; Keye was an active sleeper. He finished his dressing, padded out and down the hall, down to the foyer and out, into the glare of the floods and the business of the workmen and apprentices.

"Is it stable?" he asked of the night supervisor, Carl Gytha. "Any difficulty?"

"None," Gytha assured him. "The engineers assure us so."

He nodded, pleased with himself, looked about him where now the bone-white marble formed the strong bend of an arch against the velvet sky and the staring eyes of the floods. While he watched, another block settled, homed by the seeker-sensor that told the crane operator it was coming down on target. It hovered. The sensor plate became aligned with its mate as it settled. Workmen hastened to strip off the paired sensors, free the fore and aft clamps, scrambling along the scaffolding. Liberated, the crane swung with ponderous grace and dipped its cable after the next block the master apprentice would designate. The clamps settled, embraced, seized, lifted.

That smoothly.

Block after block, through the night. The operation had smoothed itself into a precision and a pace which held without falter; shifts worked and rested in alternation, enjoyed food and warm drink, cups which sent curls of steam up into the air. Herrin savored the hot sweet liquid, fruited milk and sugar, which fueled the crews and, keeping them off stronger drink, kept their perceptions straight and their reflexes instant. They were bright-eyed and enthusiastic, pampered by the project, afforded whatever they reasonably desired while *on* the project and promised a bonus if it met deadline, and wherever Herrin walked there was a flurry of zeal and an offering of respect.

"I'm not great, sir," an older worker said to him, when he inquired the view of the man, who had been rigging scaffolding. "But this thing is real and it's going to go on standing here and I'll look at those stones and remember doing them."

That was to him a tremendous insight, first into the thinking of the less than brilliant, with whom he had had little association and less conversation; and secondly, into possibilities and levels of the sculpture's reality which he had himself hardly yet grasped. "Indeed," he said, sucking in his breath, stirred by the concept of others falling within this design of his making. "Do you know—what *is* your name?"

"John Ree, sir," said the worker, jamming uncertain hands into his pockets as if seeking refuge for them. He was a big man, graying and weathered from work out of doors. "Ree."

"John Ree. It occurs to me to make a great bronze plaque when all's done; to set the name of every hand that worked to rear this sculpture, the apprentices, the stonemasons, the crane operators, the runners, every single one . . . out before the north wall."

"Would be splendid, sir," Ree murmured, looking confused, and Herrin laughed, walked away with energy in his step.

Within the hour, before dawn, the word had traveled. Supervisor Carl Gytha had heard, and asked him. "Everyone," he confirmed, "every name," and watched Gytha's eyes grow round, for Gytha was competent and knew at least a degree of ambition within the University.

"Yes, sir," the supervisor said earnestly.

"Make a list; keep it absolutely accurate. Cross check with Leona Pace."

"Yes, *sir*."

"To the least. To the sweepers. *Everyone*."

"Yes, sir." Gytha went off. Herrin smiled after him, marvelously self-content. "Come *on*," he heard yelled from the top of the courses, workers exhorting each other. No different

than had been . . . but was there yet a sudden keenness in
the voice?

He sculpted lives, and intents. Promised John Ree a place
in time, along with Waden Jenks and Herrin Law. Created
. . . in John Ree . . . a possibility which had never been
there in his wildest fancies.

See, John Ree would say to his son or daughter, to his children's children, *see . . . there. There I am.*

I.

Ambition . . . for ten thousand years of that unremarkable
worker's descendants. And what might it not do?

He felt a sudden lassitude, physical impact of half a night
awake, as he considered creative energies expended, looked at
the dawning which began to pale the glare of lamps, realized
what sleep he had missed. But the brain was awake, seldom
so much awake. He paced a time longer, finally knew that he
was exhausted, and headed outward, through the developing
maze of the shells, out into the pink daylight.

A row of dark figures stood there, robes flapping in the
slight breeze. Eight, nine of them, all in a row vaguely artistic—an arc observing the arc of the dome itself, he realized;
invisibles, all of them. Watching. He stopped, unease
touching him like the touch of the wind, and on an impulse
he turned and walked back through the maze to the *other*
side, the other gateway, to the south.

There were more invisibles, and more than one row, not
appearing to have any symmetry to their standing, but symmetrical all the same, because they were focused on the
dome.

He refused the sight. He turned and retraced his steps, the
way he had started in the first place. Workers called out to
each other, still shouting instructions. He swept through the
dome, out past the line of watchers, managing this time not
to see them, except as shadows.

He made no particular haste, walking in the dawning up
through the street, on which morning walkers were beginning
to appear, ordinary citizens. *Safe,* the thought came to
him, and why he should subconsciously reckon hazard he did
not know. There had never been any hazard from invisibles.
It was fancy, imagination, and he thought that he had purged
fear of that.

He moved to the Residency that morning. It was a matter

of packing up a sackful of clothing and personal items from the studio and appearing at the Residency entry desk in the main hall, casting himself on Waden's recommendation and the staff's invention. The room turned out to be extravagant, by his standards, with white woodwork and a wide, soft bed. It had a magnificent view of the Port Street walkway, the hedge, the grand expanse of Main beyond, and most important, the dome, the Work.

He was delighted, grandly pleased, stood smiling into the daylight which was streaming over distant Jenks Square.

He did not delude himself that Keye would come here. She had an almost superstitious fear of being inside this place. He grinned with amusement. So much for Keye's fears, and his twilight nightmares and watchers about the square.

So much for any assumption Keye might now make that she had dissuaded him from this venture into the Residency. He had, he thought, delayed overlong on her account . . . or his own comfort. It was, after all, a mere change of address. And Keye's apartment was still accessible from the Square . . . when there was time. He foresaw a time of increasing preoccupation, when he would not indeed have time to have made the shift to the Residency, and he would not have Keye pouring her own opinions into his ear without also doing what he chose on the contrary tack. That Keye should know his independence . . . he had no vanity in that regard—in fact whatever she wanted to think was very well, and better if she deceived herself—but he would not be dissuaded by her, or oppose her for its own sake, which was likewise to move at her direction. It was simply a good morning to get around to the move, when he could do so without particular reason one way or the other.

He found it even more pleasant than he had thought.

The door opened uninvited. "Welcome," said Waden's voice from behind him.

He turned, raised brows. "Well. It's splendid hospitality, First Citizen."

"It's nothing too good for you, is it?

"Of course not."

Waden laughed softly. "Breakfast?"

"Gladly."

"You choose strange hours for moving."

"Convenient to my schedule."

Waden's eyes traveled over him minutely. "You worked all night? Zeal, Artist."

"I enjoy my work."

"Doubtless you do."

Waden walked to the window, turned, wiped a finger across the brooch he wore on his collar, smiled quizzically. "Bizarre ornament."

Herrin smiled, said nothing, which brought a spark of amusement to Waden's eyes. Herrin laid a hand on Waden's back, turned him toward the door. "Fellows' Hall?"

Waden agreed. They walked together, ate together; Waden went back to his offices and his work; Herrin went back to his, in the studio, at peace with his reality. He gathered up his own cutter for the first time since the project began, selected his tools, went out to the Square on the nervous energy which had fired him since midway through the night.

The cranes groaned and ground their way about their business. Leona Pace came up with her checklist to see if there was anything that wanted doing; he refused her, waved off a question about the plaque and the proposal of the names to be engraved there.

"True," he said simply, and knelt down and began unwrapping his tools, his own, which were the finest available, before the pillar which would be the central sculpture. He was sure now. That had been the reason for the lack of sleep, the anxiety, the energy which had suffused him and dictated so many shiftings and changes and readjustments in recent days.

He focused himself now on his own phase of the work. The cranes hefted enormous weights which sailed like clouds overhead, any one of which, slipping, could have crushed him to grease, but he refused even the slight concern the possibility suggested.

He focused the beam, and began, oblivious to all else.

XVI

Student: Is there reality outside Freedom?
Master Law: I imagine that there is.

He dropped the cutter, finally—saw his hand was wobbling and jerked it away from the stone before disaster could happen. It fell, and he sank down where he was, dropped head into arms and arms onto knees and sat there, aware finally that he was getting wet, that rain was splashing onto his shoulders and beginning to slick all the exposed stonework. He was not cold yet, but he was going to be. His joints felt as if the tendons had all been cut and there was fire in his shoulders and his arms and his legs.

A plastic wrap fell about his shoulders. Leona Pace was there, her plump freckled face leaning down to look at him sideways. "All right, sir?"

He drew a breath, massaged his hands, nodded, looked up past Pace to the Shape which had begun in recent days to emerge from the stone, which had begun, with the beam-cutter's swift incisions, to *be* Waden Jenks. He sat there, with the rain slicking down his forehead and into his eyes, and stared at what he had done, numb already in the backside and with a grateful numbness creeping into his exposed hands.

Leona Pace followed his stare, looked down again. "It's amazing, sir."

"I should have rested." He tried for his feet, wrapping the plastic about him, and Pace made a timid effort to steady him; it gave him equilibrium. Other workers and apprentices had sheltered in the curve of an arch. The lights had come on as the clouds darkened. He turned full about, saw a dry spot under a curve and went to it, thinking Pace was following. But when he looked back she was walking away, her brown hair straggling as usual, her bearing matter-of-fact and lonely-looking.

He was spent, as from a round of sex. He felt the same melancholia as encounters with Keye tended to give him; he looked reflexively toward the window where Keye might be, and saw nothing because of the curve. The new reality was closing in. Permanent. Strangely he felt no more desire for Keye, for anyone, for anything.

And as after sex, it would return. He leaned against the stone, watching the sheen of water flow this way and that. It was the first time the work had stopped, the only circumstance which could delay it. He looked up at the sky, which was already showing signs of breaking sunlight. Such storms came and left again with suddenness in this season. The stone would dry within a short time when the rain had stopped.

The hot-drink cart made the rounds; an hour's rest became holiday. Laborers tucked up in plastics, drinking the steaming cups which splashed with raindrops, came from their shelters to stand and stare at the central sculpture, and Herrin, his own hands clasped about warm ceramic and his belly warmed by the drink, watched with vast satisfaction.

Laborers asked questions; apprentices swelled with importance and answered, pointing to the imaginary vault of the roof, the future placement of curtain-columns, and laborers explained to other laborers . . . Herrin watched the whole interchange and drank in the excitement which suffused the whole crew.

Pride. They were *proud* of what they were doing. They had come here diverse, and something strange had begun to happen to all of them in this shell, contained in this sculpture of his devising.

And then the Others came.

They filed in through the gateways and stood about, four at first and then more, midnight-robed. Ten, twelve, fifteen.

The workers *saw* them. The excitement which had been palpable before their coming tried to maintain itself, but there was an erosion, a silence, an unease. Men and women tried to maintain equilibrium, realities, *choice*. Herrin leaned against the stone and looked elsewhere, trying to ignore all of it, but they came from the other side as well.

"*Out!*" Leona Pace cried, shocking the almost-silence. Shocking every reality into focus.

She had *seen. Admitted* seeing. Her reality had slipped, and Herrin stood transfixed and helpless.

The same look was on Leona Pace—rigidity, panic. Suddenly she cast off the plastic mantle and left, running.

He kept staring at the hole where Pace had been when she passed the gateway; and the cold from the rain crept inward. He recovered after a breath, walked out casually among the workers and the invisibles, ignored what they should not see, and quietly dismissed them.

"The rain may continue," he said. "Things will have to dry. Secure the area and go home. Come back at your next regular shift."

Tools were put away against invisible pilferage; the cranes were shut down and locked; and one by one and several at a time, the workers and the apprentices drifted away.

"Andrew Phelps." He hailed the senior apprentice. "You have a responsibility next shift, to be here early, to keep accounts, to direct."

"Sir," the man said, youngish, dark and thin, his eyes still showing distress, which rapidly yielded to surprise. "Yes, sir."

So he replaced Leona Pace.

He had no illusions that she would return. It happened, he reasoned, because of the sculpture; for that moment, humans and Others had had a common focus, had gathered within the same Reality, and Leona Pace had been thrust into the center of it, responsible.

Had broken under the weight of it. Would not be back, either on the site or at the University or indeed, among sane citizens. No one would see her, just as they did not see other invisibles. Survival was for the strong-minded, and she had not been strong enough.

He drank himself numb after a moderate dinner at Fellows' Hall, walked through the slackening rain to the Residency, just barely able to steer himself to his room without faltering.

He slept and woke at the first light of another day, still lying where he had lain when he fell into bed; he bathed, assumed sober Student's Black and walked the distance to the Square; he set matter of factly to work and so did everyone else, wounds healed.

Leona Pace did not, of course, return. The cheerfulness of the crew did. Andrew Phelps was an energetic and intelligent supervisor, and that was sufficient. He did not care for the past day, revised time and his Reality and recommenced his carving with full attention to the moment.

The Shape emerged further under his hands. It was slow now, very slow. Above him, the cranes labored, and he worked in the shadow of scaffolding and stone which had sealed off the sky once and for all.

XVII

Apprentice: Which is superior, reason or creativity?
Master Law: Neither.

The scaffolding in days after was lowered again to permit work on the detailing of the triple shell, and there was solid stone overhead. There was no more sound from the cranes, which had filled the center of Kierkegaard with their groaning and grinding for what had begun to seem forever; their job was done. The crane operators took their leave, returning now and again as other jobs or simply the course of coming and going through Kierkegaard took them through the dome.

Most of the workers of other sorts were discharged with their bonuses, only a few kept for the labor of clearing away the dust and the fragments. It was work for the skilled apprentices now.

For weeks the dome remained dark except for the lights which shone inside it. And then the perforations of the innermost shell revealed the lacery which had been made by apprentices burrowing wormlike between the second and outermost shells, and light began to break upon the interior, flowing moment by moment in teardrops and shafts across the pavings and the curtain-pillars and upon the walls of the shells . . . and upon the central pillar, where the stonework became the uplifted countenance of Waden Jenks, which became first calm and then, as the hours passed and the light angles changed, shifted.

Watchers came. Citizens passed time watching and from time to time invisibles strayed through . . . few, and tolerable, a momentary chill, like the passing of a cloud; at times Herrin truly failed to notice, rapt at his work, until the shadow of a robe swept by. It was inconsequential. He paid far more attention to the shadowing of a brow, to the small indentation at the corner of the mouth, to the detailed modeling of illusory hair which swept to join the design itself. He worked and sometimes after work must straighten with caution, as if his bones had assumed permanently the position his muscles had held for hours, ignoring pain, ignoring warmth and cold, until sometimes one of the apprentices had to help him from the position in which he had frozen himself.

"It's beautiful," one said, who was steadying him on his feet, on the platform. Gentle hands, careful of him. "It's *beautiful,* sir."

He laughed softly, because it was the only word that could came to the man's tongue; *beautiful* was only one aspect of it. But he was pleased by the praise. He got down from the platform, which was a man's height from the ground, was steadied by another apprentice who waited below, with a group of others, and there was a pause among the workers, a small space of silence.

It struck him that this had *been* going on, that at times they did pause when he walked through, or when he was in difficulty, or when he began work or when he stopped.

"What are you doing?" he asked roughly. "Back to work." His back hurt still; he managed to- straighten, and heads turned. He looked back and met the faces of the apprentices who had been helping him, eyes anxious and unflinching from his outburst. He shook off their further assistance and walked on, flexed aching hands and turned to look back at the Work, which was bathed in the play of light from the trilevel perforations of the dome.

He took in his own breath, held for the moment in comtemplation.

Not finished yet. The central work was not finished. The outer shells were all but complete. Apprentice after apprentice had been sent off. Perhaps, he thought, he should acknowledge those departures, offer some tribute; he realized he

was himself the object of a second silence, all the heads
which had formerly turned to feign work turned back again.

"Good," he said simply, and turned and walked away.

It took him at least through dinner each night to get the
knots out of his muscles. It was not just the hands and back;
every joint in his body stiffened, every muscle, from the
greater which held his arm steady to the tiny one of a toe
which had been balancing him, rigidly, his whole body a
brace for his hand which held the cutter, for hour after hour,
without interruption. He had given up on lunch; often omitted breakfast because once awake he had not the patience to
divert himself to eat; dinner was all there was left, and he
had his plate of stew at Fellows' Hall, and a second and a
drink which helped ease his aches and relax his muscles . . .
not too much any longer. It had occurred to him that such a
regime might utimately affect his coordination and his
health; he attempted moderation. He sat in Fellows' Hall at
dinnertime, in Student's Black well dusted with white marble
dust, and swallowed savory food which he did not fully taste
because his mind was elsewhere, and drank cold beer which
was more relief because of the temperature than because he
tasted it. He saw little of where he was, perceived instead the
dusting of marble, the cutting of the beam, the image itself,
as if it were indelibly impressed on his retinas, persisting even
here. He walked back to the Residency and without noticing
the desk and the night guard on duty there, walked to his
room and stripped off the dusty Black to bathe in hot water,
to soak the aches out, to wrap himself in his robe against the
chill and look a last time out the window. He gazed on the
night-floods and the dome far beyond the tall hedge of Port
Street, the lighted dome resting there as the bright heart of
Kierkegaard. This he did always before going to bed . . . no
reason, except that his thoughts went in that direction, and it
was more real to him than the room was; more real than the
Residency, than any other thing about him. He looked to
know, to set his world in order, because it *was* there, and
seeing it made the day worth the pain.

He looked his fill, and started for the bed, with his eyes
and his mind full of the Work, seeing nothing about him, his
thoughts occupied wholly with the alteration which he had to
make tomorrow, which could only be made when the sun

passed a certain mark, and he had to *see* in advance, and do the cutting then.

There was a knock at the door.

It took him a moment, to blink, to accept the intrusion. Waden. No one else ever disturbed him here. He knew no one else in the Residency . . . and in fact, no one else in the city ever called on him.

"Waden?" he invited the caller without even going that way; and the door opened.

It was, of course. Waden walked in, casual-suited, in the Student's Black he affected at some hours and on some days. "Sorry. Ill?"

"Tired." Herrin sat down in one of the chairs, reached to the convenient table to pour wine from a decanter, two glasses. Waden took his and sat down. "Social call?" Herrin asked, constrained to observe amenities.

"I haven't seen you in two weeks."

Herrin blinked, sipped, sat holding the glass. "That long?"

"I see . . ." Waden made a loose gesture toward the nighted window. "*That*. From my office upstairs. I get reports."

Games. Herrin refused to ask, to plead for reaction, which Waden would surely like, that being the old game between them. He simply raised his glass and took another slow sip.

"They talk," Waden said, "as if you're really doing something special out there."

"I am."

Waden smiled. "And on budget. Amazing."

"I told you what we'd need."

"I could wish for equal efficiency elsewhere . . . Am I keeping you from . . . someone?"

"No." Herrin almost laughed. "I'm afraid I'm quite dull lately. Preoccupied."

"Not seeing Keye?"

He shook his head.

"What, a falling out?"

"No time." He had not, in fact, *realized* that he had not seen Keye in the better part of two months. He had simply postponed events. Waden, Keye, whatever had been important before . . . waited. He was amazed, too, to realize that so much time elapsed, like someone disturbed from a long sleep. "I'm afraid I haven't been social at all. To try to hold the details in my memory . . . you understand . . . it shuts out everything else."

"Details."

"Perhaps you don't understand. Your art is different, First Citizen."

" 'Not creative.' I recall your judgment. I am capable of such concentration; I currently have nothing that demands it; the limits of Freedom do not exercise me."

Herrin raised a quizzical brow, drained his glass, added more. "I heard a shuttle land last week."

"Two weeks ago," Waden laughed, and chuckled. "You *are* enveloped, Artist. Are you really that far from consciousness? A shuttle, a considerable volume of trade, a fair deal of traffic on Port Street, and none of this reached you."

"It made no shortage of anything *I* needed."

"You *are* master of your reality," Waden mocked him. "And it's all made of stone."

"No," Herrin said softly, "*your* reality, First Citizen. You are my obsession."

"An interesting fancy."

"*Should* I have noticed?"

"What, the shuttle?"

"*Should* it have been of interest to me?"

Waden smiled and refilled his own glass. "A man who forgets his personal affairs would hardly think it of interest, no. It was a military landing, Artist. There's a campaign on. They were interested in *Singularity's* itinerary. I've opened negotiations with them. I happen to have years of McWilliams's past records, cargo, statistics on all the pirates. The military is very interested. But that's very far from you, isn't it?"

"What negotiations?" he was genuinely perplexed. Waden had come here for a reason, bursting with something pent up. He drew a deep breath and looked Waden in the eyes. "Let me venture a guess. Your ministers and your departments are beyond their depth and you have no confidence in them. This is no casual call."

"Your intelligence surpasses theirs."

"Of course it does; it surpasses *yours*, but of course you have no intention of admitting it. What have you gotten yourself into?"

For a moment there was a baleful look in Waden's brown eyes, and then humor. "Indulge your fancies. They're of no consequence. You're only moderately wrong, my Dionysus: rationality is always superior to impulsive acts, even creative ones. But no, I don't want your advice; I don't need it."

"What do you need?"

Waden laughed. "Nothing, of course. But possibly what I've always needed, a little less solitude. Already you relieve my mind. I've shaken the world, Artist, and you've not even felt the tremors; what marvelous concentration you have."

"Have you taken sides?"

"Ah. To the point and dead on. Negotiations: Freedom will always be commercially poor so long as it relies on piratical commerce. And I am too great for this world."

"What have you done?"

"What would you do, as Waden Jenks?"

"Build this world. You're about to swallow too much, First Citizen. Digest what you have already; what more do you need, what—?" He lifted a hand toward the roof and the unseen stars. "What is *that?* Distances that will add to the vacancy you already govern. Hesse is still uncolonized. Half this world is vacant. What need of more so soon? Your ambition is for *size*. And you will swallow until you burst."

Waden Jenks tended to laugh at his advice, to take it in humor. There was no humor in Waden now.

"I will jar your Reality, Artist. Come with me. Come. Let me show you figures."

Herrin sucked in his breath, vexed and bothered and inwardly disturbed already; arguments with Waden were not, at this stage, productive of anything good. "My Reality is what I'm doing out there, First Citizen. Don't interfere with my work. I have no time to be bothered with trivialities."

Waden's eyes grew darker, amazed, and then he burst out laughing. "With trivialities! O my Dionysus, I love you. There's all a universe out there. There's scale against which all your ambition is nothing; there are places you'll never reach, peoples who'll never hear of you and never care, and you're *nothing*. But you shut that out, no different from the citizen who sweeps the streets, who has all the Reality he can handle."

"No. You'll give it all to me. That's what you're for. You asked me what *I* would do. I'd build up this world and attract the commerce you say we have to have. You're looking for a quick means, because Waden Jenks has no duration, only breadth. You'll devour everything you can, First Citizen, and those same people beyond your reach will always gall you; but not me. Because someday . . . at some time however far away . . . someone who's known *my* work will get out there, and carry my reputation there, and in *time*, in time, First Citizen—when we're both gone—I'll get there. My way."

"Will you?" Waden's grin looked frozen for the moment, and Herrin, wine-warmed, felt a little impulse of caution. "A little time *giving* orders has improved your confidence, hasn't it? I neglect to mention your program would simply build an economy the pirates would delight to plunder. We have *one* commodity now which we have to sell: the pirates themselves, which will buy us what will save us great expense. But I did invite comment. Plan as you choose. You've taught me something."

"What, I?"

"That duration itself is worth the risk; and that's my choice as well, Artist. By what I do . . . neither Freedom nor other worlds will go unshaken."

"Whom have you dealt with?"

"The trade . . . we can't get from merchants. But there's more than one way to get it, isn't there? The military wants a base in this sector; wants to build a station, to do for us what would take us generations. So I give them our cooperation. And Camden McWilliams ceases to annoy us."

"You've cut us off from the only commerce we get," Herrin exclaimed. "They'll desert you, this foreign military. They'll leave you once they've got what they want. They'll *change* things here, impose their own reality, never mind yours."

Waden shook his head.

"You're confident," Herrin said. "Do you really think you can handle them? It's *wide*, Waden."

"Does it daunt *you?* You talk about posterities. Does that length of time daunt you? And does it occur to you that what I do cannot be without effect in duration as well as breadth?"

"It occurs to me," he admitted.

"You never fail me," Waden said. "Whenever I'm in the least perplexed, you're the best reflection of my thoughts. My unfailing mirror. Arguing with you is like arguing with myself."

"You no longer have to flatter, First Citizen. Do you merely flex your unpracticed talents?"

"Oh, excellent. Still barbed. What of that masterwork of yours? Shall I come to see it?"

"Not yet. When it's done."

"What, afraid of my reaction?"

"When it's done."

"When will that be?"

Herrin shrugged. "Possibly a week."

"So soon?"

"Before deadline. I have had outstanding cooperation."

"I've heard you plan a tribute to the workers."

"Out of my account."

"No, no, the State will fund it."

"*Will* you? That's quite generous."

"A gesture seems in order. An inspiration to the city. I'm really impressed, Herrin, truly I am. I have administrators accustomed to such tasks of coordinating workers and supply who find less success. You have a certain talent there too, by no means minor."

"I should not care to exercise it. My sculpture is the important thing. I credit my choice of supervisors."

"One lost. Most unfortunate."

Herrin fidgeted and recrossed his ankles, feet extended before him. The reference was in total bad taste.

"An invisible."

"One supposes," Herrin said. "I'm sure I don't know."

"You're a disturbance," Waden said.

"Do I disturb you?"

Waden tossed off the rest of his drink, set the glass down, still smiling. "I shall expect to see this wonder of yours next week. Dare I?"

"Barring rain. I don't fancy working in the wet."

"Ah, you're admirably restrained. You're dying for me to see it, and probably a little apprehensive."

"Not in the least apprehensive."

"But anxious."

"I should imagine the same of you."

"True," Waden said. "True. I'll leave you to your rest. I see you were on the verge." He tapped the decanter with his fingernail. "You ought not to indulge so much. I hate to see a great mind corrupted."

"Only on occasions. I've reformed since my Student days."

"Have you?" Waden rose, and Herrin did. Waden brushed his clothes into order. "A pleasant rest to you."

"Thank you."

Waden started out. Stopped, halfway to the door, looked back. "Keye's well. Thought I'd tell you."

"My regards to her."

Waden registered mild surprise. "Bastard! Did you know?"

"She is with you, then."

"Ah, she visits. Says you've gone strange."

Herrin shrugged. "A matter of indifference to me."

"Do you know, I think she prefers you."

"Again a matter of indifference. Beware of Keye."

"Do you think so?"

"Creative ethics, Waden. She'll create yours for you; doubtless she's doing so at the moment. But that's your problem."

"Ah, you are offended."

"I'm not offended." He folded his arms to take the weight off his shoulders. His eyes were growing heavy from the drink. "I'm far too weary to cope with Keye, and she'll drift back again. Or back and forth. I'm quite surprised you two haven't reached an arrangement long before this. Evidently she feels herself in one of her stronger periods; she avoided you once; now she avoids me. I've always thought you underestimated her." A thought came to him and he penetrated his lethargy with a more direct look. "Ah! you've talked to Keye about this—plan, this ambition of yours. And lo, Keye is *with* you."

"Worth considering."

"Indeed it is."

Waden gnawed his lip, laughed softly. Nodded. "Warning taken, Herrin. Warning assuredly taken."

He left. Herrin walked to the bed and sat down, utterly weary, disturbed in his concentration. He had not asked for disturbances. What had been contentment deserted him.

He tried to put it all from his mind, revise the time, wipe it all out and start over. He failed. He was muddled, vaguely and irrationally, knowing Keye was *not* sitting in her apartment over the Square waiting for his attention. He was hurt. Of course she would not wait. Of course there was no reason that she should. He would have had no objection had she taken a horde of others to her bed. She had done so, in fact, while taking him on convenient days.

But Waden. *Waden,* who rivaled him. He took that maneuver seriously. The three greatest minds in all Freedom . . . and always Keye had maintained at least neutrality, with the balance tipped toward him. Waden conceived ambition and the Ethicist went to him like iron to a magnet.

When *his* great work was almost complete.

That desertion hurt, and the news of it had to come when he was tired, when his maintenance of his reality could be shaken. There was a cure for that. He got up, walked to the table and poured his abandoned glass full of wine. He sat down and he drank, and when he could no longer navigate steadily, he headed for bed, to lie with the lights on because he was too muddled to turn them out, with a confusion of anger in hin that was not going to accept things as they were and an exhaustion too great to think his way out of it.

He slept, more a plummet into oblivion than a sinking into rest. And he waked, leaden-limbed and with a blinding headache. He lay abed until he could no longer ignore the day, then rolled out gingerly, bathed, which diminished the headache and finally cured it.

Thinking . . . was in abeyance. He toweled off, dressed, held out his hands to see if they were steady, and they were.

Possibly, he thought—because his mind *was* most brilliant—the restlessness at night would get worse. He thought of what Waden feared—the same perspective, to have no one equal, anywhere. To be throwing out thoughts and ideas which no one could criticize because there was no one competent to comprehend.

Life without walls. With endless, endless outpouring of ideas, and nothing coming back, being at the center of everything, and radiating like a star . . . into void.

To be cursed with increasing intellect, and increasing comprehension of one's reality, and increasing grasp. . . .

You'll swallow, he recalled saying to Waden Jenks, *until you burst.*

That was not, he thought, what Waden feared. It was rather expansion . . . until expansion became attenuation, became dissipation . . . until Waden had never been.

A wave with no shore.

The thought began to occur to him as well. As it might

have occurred to Keye. He had left Keye alone, without a shore to break the wave, and she had gone to Waden; as Waden went to him when Keye did not suffice.

And where now did Herrin Law go?

To deaden his mind every night because the thoughts were too vivid and the brain too powerful, so powerful that the only way to deal with it was to anesthetize it, to get null, for a few precious hours?

Until the machine tore itself apart?

The hands were steady at the moment. He had that confidence, at least.

XVIII

Waden Jenks: Your hubris surpasses mine.
Master Law: Philosophy argues that hubris doesn't exist.
Waden Jenks: But it does. There are offenses against the State.
Master Law: I purpose nothing against the State.
Waden Jenks: No, your ambition is far greater.

He decided on breakfast, to be kind to his abused body, to guard his health, food was a good cure for such moods. Well-being generally restored his confidence. He left for the University dining hall rather than order breakfast up from Residency kitchens, which could take far longer than it was worth, which was why he had given up on breakfasts, when he thought about it. He considered his physical condition, which was approaching excessive attrition; hours of physical labor on small intake and limited sleep. Food at regular hours had to help.

He was, in fact, stripped of resolve, of the energy which had sustained him thus far. He ate a far larger breakfast than he had ever been accustomed to since childhood, full of sugars and washed down with milk; he asked the kitchen to pack him a cold lunch, which he took with him in a paper bag; and he walked at a slow pace toward Jenks Square, letting breakfast settle.

He did, he concluded, feel better for all these measures of self-improvement. He walked along the street noticing his surroundings for the first time in weeks.

And invisibles were there.

He flinched from that realization. The first one he saw was where Second intersected Main, coming from a corner, and perhaps there had been others all along, but *after* this one there were others, farther down the street.

Another difficulty of a brain which could not be shut down. Perception. *He* saw them. And what should he ask of others who had been born in Kierkegaard? *Do* you *really see them?* They were there, that was all. He had not put on the brooch this morning—hubris did not go with his mood—now he was desperately glad that he had not. He no longer felt like challenging anything.

One cloaked, hooded figure had stopped, and he stopped. It was Leona Pace.

He stood there perhaps half the beat of his heart, and flinched, walked on past as he ought. The midnight robes, which blanked both ahnit and invisible human from the view of the sane, veiled a shoulder, a blankness.

Perhaps it was the shock he needed to jar him from his private misery, that sight of a reality fractured, a fine talent lost, the waste, the utter waste of it. He did not look back.

The dome lay before him, the vision which made all other things trivial. *This* was the thing, this beautiful object, on which he had poured out all his energy for months, which had taken on shape and life and form. To have it finished, to have it be what it was meant to be . . . was worth the Leona Paces and the pain of his own body. Was worth everything, to have this in existence, shining in the morning, the sun sheening the stone with the illusion of dawn-color, with the interior now opened and hinting at convolutions within. It glowed with interior light at the moment, because they had not yet shut down the inside lights which the night crews used, bright beads gleaming in the perforations.

He walked within, where steps and taps on stone echoed, where voices spoke one to the other, hidden in the huge triple shell and the curtain-walls and bent about by acoustics and the size of the place. Some of the echo effect he had planned; some was serendipitous, but beautiful: the place rang like a bell with voices, purified sounds, refined them as it refined the the light and cast it in patterns. It took chaos and made symphony; glare and made beauty.

The center, beyond the devolving curtain-pillars, held the scaffolding, the image, still shrouded in metal webbing.

And he stopped, for crews were gathered there, both crews, and both supervisors, Gytha and Phelps; the apprentices, the workers, everyone . . . more coming in until there could be no one of the active workers omitted, past or present.

"Done?" he asked. His own voice echoed unexpectedly in their hush, which was broken only by the human stirring of a quiet crowd. "Is it finished?"

Carl Gytha and Andrew Phelps brought their tablets, the daily and evening ritual, and another brought an armload of computer printout, the maps from which they had worked, all solemnly offered. He signed the tablets, looked about him at all of them, somewhat numb at the realization that for most of them there was nothing now to do.

"*Well* done," he said, because saying something seemed incumbent on him. "*Well* done."

There was a murmur of voices, as if this had somehow been what they wanted to hear. He was bewildered by this, more bewildered when apprentices and workers simply stood there . . . and finally Gytha and Phelps offered their hands, which he took, one after the other.

"Go," he said. "I've some finishing. I'll still need a small crew; Gytha, Phelps, you stay to assist. Pick a handful. The rest of you—it's *done*."

He winced at the applause, which multiplied and redoubled like madness in the acoustics of the dome. He nodded in embarrassment, not knowing what else to do, turned matter-of-factly to his platform and his tools, and took off his kit with his lunch and set that down; scrambled up with the agility of practice, and set himself to work.

Confusion persisted. People stayed to talk, and voices and steps echoed everywhere. This failed to distract him, rather calmed him, because it was the life he had planned for the Work, that the interior should live, that there should be people, and voices, and laughter and living things flowing through it.

Eventually the noise changed, from the familiar voices to the strange voices of citizens, but the tone of it was much the same. There was, occasionally, a soft whisper of wonder, the piercing voice of a child trying out the echoes; but the scaffolding wrapped the centermost piece, the heart of it, and his activity fascinated those who stood to watch him work. "Hush," his remaining assistants would say. "Hush, don't bother him." And: "That's Herrin Law. That's the Master." He ignored those voices and the others, much more rapt in the consideration of an angle, the waiting, the aching waiting, for the right moment, as the afternoon sun touched precisely the point of concern, and he had a very small time to make the precise stroke which would capture one of the statue's changing expressions without destroying all the rest of the delicate planes.

This day and the next and the next he labored, now with abrasive and polish, now smoothing out the tiniest rough spots. It rained, and he worked, until Gytha came and wrapped a warm cloak about him and got him off the platform; and others were there, who had not been there, he thought, in days, wrapped in their own rain gear and bringing raincoats with them. "I thought he might need it," one said. "He doesn't take care of himself," said another, female.

He looked at them askance, huddled within Gytha's cloak. He was offered warm drink, coddled and surrounded by dozens more who had come, some with blankets and some with warm drink. "Well," said one, "it's raining outside; we might as well share the drink and wait."

And another: "*Look* at it," in a tone of awe, but he was looking toward the statue, not the storm. "Look at it," another echoed, and despite the water which dripped in curtains through the apertures, a thousand tiny waterfalls, they moved to see.

Herrin watched them, drank and sat down where it was comfortable, warmed by their presence as much as any physical offering. John Ree was there, and Tib and Katya . . . he knew all their names, every one. They were artists and stonemasons and cranemen and runners, all sorts; and there was a strangeness about them as they sat down and shared their drink and their raincoats and sent their voices echoing through the curtain-walls.

It was the sculpture, Herrin thought suddenly. It was that

which had taken them in, seized them by the emotions, a reality more powerful than theirs. He shivered, recalling the Others, and Leona Pace, the day they had been trapped into seeing each other, because sane and invisible had had, here, a common focus.

The effect went on. It kept drawing them back. Those who had been *in* the Work belonged to it; sane, prideful people began to lose their realities as surely as the invisibles lost their own. The Work did not let them go. He thought that he should warn them. And then he tried to analyze his own impulse in that direction and suspected *that*.

These people frightened him. Perhaps they frightened each other. He wanted to have things *done,* and it was all but finished. He had to look elsewhere, to other things, to the rest of his reality. And that was where the rest of them had failed. They could not make the break.

"I think," he confided to them, and voices fell silent and faces turned to him, "that we can take down the scaffolding tomorrow, all the lights, clean it and sweep it and prepare it . . . It's complete. It's finished. But—" Their watching faces haunted him. He groped for something less final, hating his weakness. "There'll be more projects. Others. Those of you who want will always have first priority when I choose crew; maybe here, maybe elsewhere. You're the best. We can do *more* than this."

"I want on," said John Ree. Voices tumbled over his, all asking. *Me, Master Law, Me.*

He nodded. "All who want." They were shameless as children. As if they were his. They stirred that kind of protective feeling in him, an embarrassment for their sakes where they had no shame. In fact they were comfortable about him, like an old garment; with them he could breathe easier, knowing things were going well without his watching, because they *were* good.

"We can get that scaffolding down," said John Ree, who was discharged and already had his pay.

Herrin nodded. "Everything but mine. There's still some polishing. That comes down . . . maybe in two days."

There were nods, tacit agreement. The drink passed; the rain splashed down. There were warmer places to sit than where they were and certainly drier, but there was laughter and good humor, people who had known each other for months discussing families and how they had gotten on and what they had done with their bonuses and whose baby was born and who had what at market and how here and there people should meet for lunch or dinner. Herrin listened, both included and excluded, taking interest in the whole biazarre situation.

Then the rain stopped and they went away again, taking their empty bottles and their tarps and wishing him well. Even some complete outsiders from the street who had sheltered here and stood amazed on the fringes of the group had gotten to talking, and bade each other farewell and in some instances invited each other to meet again on the streets as if they knew each other.

And quietly, a lingering echo, the wet tap of footsteps which had been behind the curtain-walls, in the outer shells; Herrin heard them, casually, because there was no reason not to. He looked, and his skin drew, because he saw Others, whose midnight cloaks were wet, who did not depart, but stood there staring.

He cleared his throat, shrugged, turned to the scaffolding and scrambled up again, taking up the polishing, which was tedious work but mindless. He dried the area with a cloth from his pocket, and took up the abrasive again, set to work, ignoring Gytha and Phelps and the others who stirred about disassembling some of the other scaffolding.

He worked until his shoulders ached, and became aware, slowly, of the presence of a shadow at the foot of the scaffold.

He looked down, drawn by a horrid fascination, fighting his own instincts, which knew, as from one night he had known, that something would be there.

The invisible was looking up. It was Leona's face framed within the midnight hood, her plump freckled face and her brown hair and her stout shape within the cloak. There was longing in her eyes, which looked up at the statue.

"Leona," he said, very, very softly, and frightened her and himself. "Are you all right, Leona?"

She nodded, almost imperceptibly. There was a vast silence. Perhaps Gytha and Phelps were looking this way. No, they could not. It was like the wearing of the brooch—people would not see it because they dared not see it, because it was not right to see. And if people went on seeing. . . .

There were solutions for the invisibles if people started seeing them. There was the Solution, which the State had always avoided; and he knew it and surely Leona Pace knew it, and he wished that he *could* look through her.

She turned and walked away. He found himself shivering as if the wetness of the wood on which he was sitting had gotten through the tarp, or the coldness of the stone traveled up his hands into his heart. He thought that perhaps he should go home for the day, rest, drive himself no further. But that was to admit that something had happened. He looked at Gytha and Phelps, when a clatter drew his attention: they were working away, and probably they had *not* noticed.

Or they were stronger than he at the moment.

He shivered and steadied his hands enough to begin his polishing again. He felt everything slipping again, everything balanced on a precipice and ready to tumble over the edge. What did the rest of his life promise if this was the beginning: brilliance, leading to madness?

There was a thunder in the sky that for the moment he attributed to the clouds and the rain, but it kept coming, and steadied, and he knew then what it was, that at the port a part of Waden's reality had come to earth. A part of his own, at some time to come. He had no time for it at the moment, did not want to think about it . . . yet. There was a cold spot where that knowledge rested, colder than the stone or the recent rain. He heard the shuttle come down and heard the noise stop. His mind kept running with the image, the prospect of Waden Jenks's offworld negotiations, the world irrevocably widening, the walls all abolished, and nothing to do but keep staring at the horizons and widening and widening forever.

He pursed his lips and dipped his cloth in the abrasive, concentrated on the curve he was smoothing, finger width by finger width.

Something stirred near him, a step. Suddenly someone reached up near him and took the hammer. *Leona,* he thought; he did not want to see. There was the impression of midnight cloth in the corner of his eye. Slowly the tool moved off the platform, and there was a crash, metal on stone; he looked, alarmed.

He stared within a blue hood at no human face, and at

once his vision blanked and he caught for support against the statue itself. It went away, a shadow in his vision, and he stayed there with his heart beating against his ribs and the impression of what he had *almost* seen lingered in his vision, wide dark eyes, a dusky color like the cloth, and features . . . he did not want to see. Ever.

"Sir?" Carl Gytha asked, coming near the platform. "You all right, sir?"

He nodded, shrugged, put himself to work again.

Simple pilferage. He finished the place he had begun, calmly set himself at the next. It had gone long enough . . . he could work late, drive himself just a little longer. . . .

. . . get finished with this, once for all.

No, he reminded himself. He had tired that and nearly broken himself. "I'm folding up," he said. "Going back for the day."

"We'll stay," Gytha said, "by turns. Keep things from harm."

They came to help him down. He accepted the help, dusted himself off and started the walk home, for a decent supper and a little rest.

They had seen, he persuaded himself. Even normal people *saw* as much as he had seen. They proved that, by offering to stay and protect things. He was not abnormal. Perhaps they had seen Leona Pace, too, and were too self-possessed to admit it. He had never been able to ask anyone. No one was able to ask anyone.

He walked as far as the hedge and through the archway. He stopped then and blinked in surprise at the entourage which had come down Port Street and pulled up in front of the Residency. There were vehicles and troops; men in no-color uniforms . . . with weapons. He had never seen the like, not in such numbers. They filled four trucks; a fifth was vacant, with soldiers all over the frontage of the Residency, and some in the doorway; and now came transports with what might be dignitaries. Those were not Kierkegaard vehicles, they had come from offworld. From up there and out there, and something larger than an ordinary shuttle had landed to carry all of that.

His appetite deserted him. He walked across the street, between the trucks, startled as one of the Outsiders swung a gun in his direction.

"Get out of here," they told him in a strange accent. He gave them a foul look and walked on to the Residency steps, stared in outrage as one of those guarding the door barred his way with an extended arm.

"I live here," he said. "Get out of my way."

The soldier looked uncertain at that, and he pushed past in that moment, found more Outsiders in the halls inside. "*You,*" said a soldier near the desk, but the regular secretary intervened. "He's Master Herrin Law."

"Master of what?" the offworlder asked.

Herrin turned a second foul look on him and the man declined further questions. "I want this lot clear of my room," he told the secretary.

"Sir," the secretary said meekly, caught between.

"I'll have supper in my room. Send the order."

"The First Citizen asked, if you should come in before midnight, sir, he's in his office, sir."

Herrin said nothing, paused for a third look at the offworlder, young and unrecommended by his manner, which would have had him eaten alive at University: from bluster he had gone to a perceptible flinching. "Not quality material," Herrin judged acidly, and walked off.

He was trembling in every muscle. Outraged.

Outsiders. Invisibles no less than Leona Pace. They were *here*, in the Residency, and Waden Jenks invited them in. He headed for the stairs, walked up the five flights of stairs and into a whole array of guards.

"Out of my way," he said, and walked through with the assumption they would not dare. One seized his arm and he glared at that man until the hand dropped.

"Excuse me, sir. Presence up here has to be cleared."

"You're incompetent and ignorant. Clear it."

"If you'll tell me who you are, sir."

"Get the First Citizen out here. Now."

The hand left his arm. The man backed off, blinked and backed a few paces to Waden's door, knocked on it. "Sir. *Sir.*"

The door opened; Herrin walked toward it and soldiers shifted in panic. A rifle barrel slammed into his arm. He kept going nonetheless, through the door before they stopped him. Waden was there, risen from his chair among others.

"Let him go," Waden said at once, and Herrin stalked in,

shedding the soldiers like so many parasites. "What is this?" Herrin asked.

"Herrin Law," Waden said, gesturing to the others. "Colonel Martin Olsen, Military Mission."

Herrin failed to follow the hand, stared at Waden instead. "The halls are cluttered. Something struck me—I call your attention to the matter."

"Citizen Law," one of the Outsiders said, offering a hand. Herrin looked past the lot of them, smiled coldly, seeing Keye standing, in Student's Black, by the wall of the ell the room made.

"Keye, how pleasant to see you. I meant to come and call. Waden explained things. I owe you profound apologies for my desertion. You distressed me; I admit it freely. I've mended my ways, you see, moved into the Residency. Are you living here or just sleeping over?"

Keye's mouth quirked into a familiar smile. "Does it concern you?"

"*Herrin.*"

He looked at Waden, read behind the slow smile which was less amused than Keye's.

"First Citizen," said the intrusive voice. "Would you explain?"

Waden ignored it too. "Point taken, Artist. But there is a certain reality operative here that *I* choose. I'll remind you of that."

"Construe it for me. I'll decide if I want to participate."

"Bear with me. Master Herrin Law, let me present Colonel Martin Olsen, with that understanding."

The hand was offered a second time. Herrin looked the stout gray-haired man up and down, finally reached and scarcely touched the offered fingers. The hand withdrew.

"Not an auspicious color," he commented of the midnight clothing.

"I agree," said Waden. "Herrin, don't be argumentative in this. A personal favor."

"There seems to have been a misunderstanding," said the colonel. "If there was some difficulty, we extend an apology."

"Second mistake," Herrin said, passing a glance past him on the way to Keye. "Are you going to wait for this or will you join me for dinner?"

"I have a commitment," she said. "Another time."

"I trust so," he said. "Waden, I reserve judgment on your Reality. What do you purpose for them?"

"Easier if you sit and join this."

"Another time." He glanced down and brushed marble dust and abrasive from his black-clad thigh. "I'm hungry; I find no prospect here."

"First Citizen," said the invisible voice, carefully modulated.

"He's a University Master," Waden said. "Colonel, I suggest you withdraw that escort of yours to the suggested perimeter immediately, and trust us for your security; the scope of this incident is wider than may appear to you."

"Go," the colonel said. Waved his hand. There was a hesitation. *"Out."* His forces began to melt away.

"I'm going to supper," Herrin said.

"Citizen Law," said the colonel. "We're anxious to have an understanding."

Herrin turned and walked to the door. "Keye, Waden," he paused to say, "good evening."

"Herrin," Waden warned him. "They will be confined to the port area."

"That is the appropriate place."

"There will be no intrusion."

"Good evening."

"Good evening, Herrin." Waden walked forward, set a hand on his shoulder, and pulled him into a gentle embrace with a pat on the arm, then let him go again. It was odd, without particular emotion, neither passionate nor personal; it was for the invisible, and Herrin suffered it with some humor, patted Waden's arm as well, exchanged a wryly amused look at Keye, and left, into a hall now deserted.

But he was disturbed at the prospect of Outsiders, and his heart was still beating quite rapidly. It was begun, Waden's work, Waden's art. He felt a residue of anger, and at the same time tried to reason it away . . . for whatever was begun in there, whatever—and at the moment he had no wish to divert himself with speculations—it meant a new policy and program which would widen more than Waden's reality: it was his own which was being expanded. Things which *he* had set in motion were simply coming into play and, he reasoned, perhaps it was as well, with his own Work almost finished, that another phase should begin unfolding. He was melancholy with a sense of anticlimax, that somehow he had expected more elation in his own accomplishment than he felt at the moment.

Keye occurred to him, a recollection of her quiet regard in that room, her understated presence . . . her silences, which warned him that whatever was underway, Keye never announced her programs, that she perhaps deluded herself of power, and might do things without warning.

What have I said to her? he wondered, but he had always been reticent. In his heart he had always known that Keye was apt to undertake such a maneuver. He had never spilled information to her which he did not ultimately destine for Waden's ears.

But he might have given her silent communications.

And she had deserted him at the moment when his own accomplishment was highest. She had never come to admire his work, not that he ever knew. She had watched it until the closing of the dome sealed it, but she had never seen the heart of it.

Had not, he supposed, wanted that influence upon her. Not yet. Perhaps she would never come; would always evade it. That evidenced a certain fear of his strength and talent. He decided so, more satisfied when he put it in that perspective. And Waden avoided it; in another kind of fear, he thought, fear of disappointment, perhaps—or the enjoyment of anticipation. He knew Waden, knew well enough Waden's unwillingness to be led; of course Waden was going to feign nonchalance at the last moment, was going to occupy himself with whatever he could and ignore him as long as he could.

He felt more and more confident. He smiled to himself as he walked down the stairs to his own apartment, a stairway now clear of strangers and invisibles.

That night he stood at the window to look out on the city and there was a darkness where before lights had shone over the dome. He missed the glow, and yet the darkness itself was a sign of completion. Generations to come might want to light the Square by night; but for his part, it belonged in the sun, which gave it essence. He turned his face from the window and paced, restless, his thoughts more toward the port than, this night, toward Jenks Square.

He took the brooch which had lain on the table, from beside the tray which the servants would take away, but no one had pilfered the brooch and he had not, in fact, expected that it would vanish. He ran his fingers over it, traced the smooth spirals of the design and the silky surface of the blue stones. Invisible, like the makers, like the mind which had shaped it and the hands which had handled it until his took it up.

And he went to the closet and clipped it to the collar of the Black he would wear tomorrow. The humor of it pleased him; he had had enough of invisible absurdities, because still the memory of that Outsider hand which had dared check him rankled. His arm felt bruised. So he chose his own absurdities. Let Waden comment. He dusted himself and stripped off his still dusty garments and tossed them into the corner, his old and own habits; the Residency had made him too meticulous, as Keye had wished to make him, observant of her amenities.

So let the servants pick it up if they liked. Servants *washed* the clothes. They could find them wherever they were dropped and he had no present desire to be agreeable to anyone. He began to weary of the Residency, this stifling place where Waden's guests came and went.

He thought of returning to the University. He thought even of Law's Valley and a visit to Camus Province, recalled that he had thought of summoning his family here for his great day, that on which the Work would be finished, but *that* . . . that indicated a desire for something, which he denied, and the mere thought of the ·logistics involved was tedium. He desired nothing; *needed* nothing. He found himself charged with a surfeit of energy, facing physical work on the morrow, but with nothing for his mind to do. He could not face bed, or sleep, and thought of Keye again, with vexation. He paced and thought even of dressing again and going out and walking the streets to burn off the energy.

He should have stayed in that conference. Waden's invisible might have been interesting. And if he had stayed, there would have been trouble, because he was in a mood for encounter, for debate, for anything to occupy his mind, and Waden and Keye *without* the visitor would have been the company he would have chosen. But he had sensed in Waden a protective attitude toward the intruder: Waden's Art . . . he did well, he decided, to have walked out, and not to have been there in his present state of energy.

He paced, and ended up at the table again, staring at the rest of the wine which had come with dinner, and reminding himself that he had decided not to take that route to sleep; that he was headed away from that very visible precipice. It damaged him. So did lying awake and rising early, and doing physical and mental labor on two hours' sleep a night.

With resentment, he uncapped the bottle, poured the glass full, set bottle and glass by the bedside.

He began to think where he *was* going next, what project he might have in mind; but the one he was finishing was still too vivid for him, refused to leave his thoughts and yet refused further elaborations. It became a pit out of which he could not climb, offering no broader perspectives, affording him no view of where he was going next.

The vision would come, he reckoned, lying abed and sipping at the wine and staring at the wall opposite, with the dark window at his left and nothing out there to dream about. It *would* come. As yet it did not.

XIX

Waden Jenks: *Inspire me, I defy you to do more.*

Master Law: *When I defy you to do more, I fear you can.*

Waden Jenks: *Then have you not, Herrin, met your master?*

Master Law: *Then have you not met the thing you say you fear most?*

The finish came at night. The Work stood complete and it was all done—in the dark and with no admirers. The night was cold as nights in the season could be, with a beclouded moon and puddles of rain in the dome, water which had drifted through the perforations as a light mist that haloed the lamps.

Herrin had seen the finish near, so near, had pushed himself on after dark. "Light," he had asked of Carl Gytha and Andrew Phelps, who remained with him; and John Ree, who was there for reasons unexplained; and some of the others who had decided to work the off shift of other jobs they had gotten since the project finished, or after classes they had joined after the finish of the project; and nighttime strollers who had found a place to be and something going on ended up lending a hand with the carrying of this and that. "Light," he would say, his back turned to all of this activity, and peevishly, for his arms ached and he had bitten through his lip from the sheer strain of holding his position to polish this place and the other. It did not occur to him to inquire whether holding that light was a strain; or it did, but he was having trouble reaching a spot at the moment and forgot to ask afterward. His own pain was by far enough, and he was beset with anxiety that he could not last, that they would face the anticlimax of giving up, and coming back at dawn to do the last work, all because *his* strength might give out. He worked, and gave impatient orders that kept the beam on the sculpture so that he could see what he was doing; he ran sore hands over the surface which had become like glass, seeking any tiny imperfection.

"We'll *do* it," they said about him, and, "Quiet, don't rattle that," and, "The foundry *has* it; we can get it. . . ." The plaque, they meant: he had asked about that, in a lull for rest, and he trusted they were doing something in the matter, because he had shown them where it should go, had picked a paving-square which could come out, out where the square began to be the Square, and not Main. They had hammered the paving-square out during the day, and prepared the matrix, not only to set the names in bronze, but to seal the bronze to protect it from oxidation and from time. He heard some activity outside, and ignored it, locked in his own concentration on his own task.

He stopped finally and took the cup a worker thrust to his lips, took it in his own aching hands, drank and drew breath.

"Get the scaffolding down now," he said, a mere hoarse whisper. "It's *done*."

"Yes, *sir*," said Carl Gytha, and patted his shoulder. "Yes, *sir*."

He swung his legs off the platform.

"It's *done*," someone said aloud, and the word passed and echoed in the acoustics of the dome . . . *done* . . . *done* . . . *done* . . . drowned by applause, a solemn and sober applause, from a whole array of people who had no obligation to be there at all. He slid down into steadying hands, and there was a rush to get him a coat and to hand him his drink, as if he were their child and fragile. "What about the plaque?" he asked, remembering that.

"In, sir," said John Ree. "Got it set and setting, and not a bubble."

"Show me."

They did, held their breath collectively through his inspection of it, which was exactly the size of one of the meter square paving blocks. It was set in and true as John Ree had said. They had lights on it to help dry the plastic. WADEN ASHLEN JENKS, the plaque said, FIRST CITIZEN OF FREEDOM, BY THE ART OF MASTER HERRIN ALTON LAW and . . . Leona Kyle Pace, Carl Ellis Gytha, Andrew Lee Phelps, master apprentices . . . Lara Catherin Anderssen, Myron Inders Andrews. . . .

The names went on, and on, and filled the surface of the plaque, down to the foundry which had cast it.

Pace. That name was there, and how it had gotten there, whether they had used an old list and no one had wanted to *see* the name to take it off before they had given it to the foundry, or no one wanted to take it off at all, or both of those things . . . it was there, and an invisible was atop the whole list of workers and apprentices. He fingered the pin he wore, tempting the vision of those about him, and nodded slowly, and looked back past the encircling crowd of those who had gathered in the dark, where light still showed inside the dome and the scaffolding was coming down.

"Let's get it all done," he said, "so the sun comes up on it whole, and finished."

They moved, and all of them worked, carrying out the pieces of the scaffolding, worked even with polishing cloths and on hands and knees, cleaning up any hint of debris or stain, polishing away any mark the scaffolding itself might have made.

The lights went out, and there was only the night sky for illumination, a sky which had begun to be clear and full of stars. Those who walked here now shed echoes, and began to be hushed and careful. The sculpted face of Waden Jenks, gazing slightly upward, took on an illusory quality in the starlight, like something waiting for birth, biding, and lacking sharp edges.

Some went home to bed, a trickle which ebbed away the bystanders, and more went home nursing sore hands and exhaustion, probably to lie awake all night with aches and pains; but some stayed, and simply watched.

Herrin was one, for a time. He looked at what he had created, and listened, and it still seemed part of him, a moment he did not want to end. Gytha and Phelps were still there. He offered his hand to them finally and walked away, out through the silent gates of the dome and into the presence of Others, who had come as they often did, harming nothing.

The silence then was profound. He looked back, and stood there a time, and enjoyed the sight, the white marble dome in the starlight, the promise of the morning.

Keye's window . . . was dark.

Not at home, perhaps.

He looked aside then, and walked on up Main, occasionally flexing a shoulder, recalling that he had missed supper. He resented the human need to eat, to sleep; there was a sense of time weighing on him. The mind, which he had vowed not to anesthetize again, was still wide awake and promised to remain so, working on everything about it, alive and alert and taking no heed of a body which trembled with exhaustion and ached with cramps. He thought of the port, with Waden's guests; of Keye, with Waden; of Pace, whether *she* might have come this night and gone away unnoticed; of Gytha and Phelps; of dinner and what it was he could force his stomach to bear; of Outside and ambitions and stations and the other continent and what he should do with that and how the morning was going to be and whether it would rain; and how he could keep going if he were to go to bed without supper, whether he could force himself to have the patience for breakfast, and how long he could keep going if he skipped both—and whether Waden Jenks, in perverse humor, would not try to make little of the day and the moment and all that he had accomplished. All this poured through his mind in an endlessly recycling rush, robbing him of any hope of sleep.

He was alone on the street; it was that kind of hour, and a chill night, and sane citizens were not given to walking by night without a purpose. He passed the arch in the hedge which led onto Port Street and remarked with tired relief that there were no Outsiders about and no prospect of meeting any.

"Tell the First Citizen I expect him at the Square tomorrow morning," he told the night secretary. "Master Law," said the secretary, "the First Citizen has it in his appointments." That relieved his mind, and when he was about to walk away, "Master Law," the secretary said to him, "is it finished?"

The interest, the question itself pleased him. "Yes," he said, and walked away, suddenly possessed of an appetite.

He slept, on a moderately full stomach, in his own bed and without the wine.

And he wakened with the sense of a presence leaning over him, stared up startled into the face of Waden Jenks.

"Good morning, Artist. What a day to oversleep, eh?"

He blinked, gathering his wits, decided no one just wakened was capable of matching words with Waden, and rolled out of bed in silence, stalked off to the bath and showered and shaved while Waden waited.

"Hardly conversational," Waden complained from the other room.

"What shall I say?" He negotiated the razor past his moving lips. "People who break into rooms shouldn't expect coherent responses. What time is it?"

"Nine. I didn't want to go without you."

"Well, I wasn't sure I'd go. After all, *my* part's done."

"You're incredible."

"Meaning you don't believe me?"

"Meaning I don't."

Herrin smiled at the mirror, ducked his head, washed off and dried his face. He walked out where Waden was standing, searched the closet for clean clothes, nothing splendid, but rather his ordinary Student's Black. Waden was resplendent in gray, expensive, elegant; but he usually was.

"You know," Waden said, watching him, "that you could *have* better than that."

"I don't take care of things like that. I forget. I start to work and ruin clothes. I'm afraid I'll never achieve elegance."

He pulled on trousers and pulled on his shirt and fastened the collar and the cuffs, sat down and put on socks and boots, all sober black.

"You really mean to wear that?"

"Of crouse I do."

"Incredible."

"I'm simply not ostentatious." He finished, stood up, and combed his hair in the room mirror . . . paused there, recalling the invisible brooch which was his private absurdity, his only ornament. He found Waden's presence intimidating in that regard, and for a moment entertained the thought that *this* day at least he should not play the joke.

No. On those terms he had to, or Waden did intimidate him.

He hunted out the clothes he had dropped the night before, unclipped the brooch and stood up, smiled at Waden, clipping it to his collar. "I'm ready to go if you are. Will Keye come?"

"She's waiting outside."

"*That's* remarkable. She's always refused. Possibly a taste for the finished and not the inchoate."

"Do you suggest so?"

"Ah, I was speaking of art."

Waden smiled tautly. "Such deprecation isn't like you. *Are* you hesitant?"

"What, to offend you? Never. You thrive on it. But we're both finished now, while before, you'd achieved and I'd done nothing. *Something* stands out there now."

"Not to win Keye's attention."

Herrin laughed. "Hardly. Keye's attentions are to herself and always have been." He opened the door, stopped because there were Outsiders there. Blue-uniformed Outsiders.

"Something wrong?" Waden asked.

Half a heartbeat he hesitated, seeing the game and still finding it early in the morning for maneuvers like this. Invisibles. He wore a brooch. Waden Jenks had attendants. He stepped aside to let Waden out and closed the door. Keye was there, sitting in a chair a little distance down the hall, reading, legs crossed and nonchalant.

"Keye," he said, and she looked up, folded the book and tucked it into her pocket, rising with every evidence of delight in the day.

"Good morning," she said.

"Good morning." He looked back at Waden. The escort was still with them. He smiled, oblivious to it all, and the three of them and their invisible companions trooped down the several turns of the stairs to the main level and out, into the pleasant sunlight.

"The light is an advantage," he said.

"I should think," said Waden.

They walked across Port Street and the escort kept with them, dogging their steps. *Notice them,* Waden defied him; Herrin drew a deep breath and strode along briskly with Keye and Waden on either side of him, but in his heart he *was* disturbed, angered that Waden had found a way to anger him, a means which he had not anticipated to try to make this day less for him than it might be. Waden was Waden and there was no forgetting that. This troublesome fragment of his own reality existed to vex him—and that Waden took such pains to vex him—was in itself amusing.

Through the archway in the hedge and onto Main itself, the escort stayed; he heard them, a rustle and a crunching step on gravel and on paving. Looking down Main even from this far away he could see an unaccustomed gathering, where the dome filled the square at the heart of Kierkegaard.

His own people would be there, of course, and by the look of it, a good many citizens . . . an amazing number of citizens. The street was virtually deserted until they reached the vicinity of the dome, and then some of the bystanders outside saw them, and the murmur went through the crowd like a breath of wind.

People moved for them, clearing them a path, and the main gateway of the dome emptied of people as the crowd moved aside to let them pass; people flowed back again like air into a vacuum, with a little murmur of voices, but before them was quiet, such quiet that only the footfalls of those retreating echoed within the dome.

"Master Law," some whispered, and, "Waden Jenks," said others; but Keye's name they did not whisper, because the ethicist was not so public; the whispers died, and left the echoes of their own steps, which slowed . . . even Herrin looked, as the others did.

Sun . . . entered here; shafts transfixed the dark and flowed over curtain-walls and marble folds, touched high surfaces and failed in low, touched the clustered heads of the crowd which hovered about the edges, the first ring, the second. . . .

And the third, where the central pillar formed itself out of the textured stone and dominated the eye. The face, sunlit, glowed, gazed into upward infinities; there was little of shadow on it. It seemed to have force in it, from inside the stone; it was hero and hope and a longing which drew at the throat and quickened the heart.

It was not Waden as he was; it was possibility. And for the first time Herrin himself saw it by daylight without the metal scaffolding which had shrouded it and let him see only a portion of it at a time. It lived, the best that Waden might be . . . and for a moment, looking on it, Waden's face took on that look, a beauty not ordinarily his; others, looking on it, had such a look—it was on Keye's face, but quickly became a frown, defensive and rejecting.

Herrin smiled, and drew in the breath he had only half taken. Smiled when Waden looked at him.

And Waden's face became Keye's, doubting. "It's remarkable, Artist."

"Walk the interior, *listen* to it, it has other dimensions, First Citizen."

Waden hesitated, then walked, walked in full circuit of the pillar, and looked at the work of the walls, let himself be drawn off into the stone curtains of the other supports and of the ring-walls. Herrin stood, and cast occasional looks at Keye, who once stared back at him, frowning uncertainly, and at the invisible escort, who had also entered here. He *knew* that they saw something remarkable, and for a moment had lost themselves in it. Waden walked temporarily unescorted; and if the escort was supposed to watch *him*, that failed too. Herrin looked beyond them, smiled in pleasure, because he saw members of his own crew, who grinned back at him.

Walking the circuit of the place, appreciating the folds and complications of it, took time. Herrin clasped his hands behind his back and waited, in the center and under everyone's eyes, until at last Waden Jenks finished his tour and came back.

Waden nodded. "Fine, very fine, Artist. But I expected that of you."

Herrin made a move of his hand toward the central pillar,

the sculpted face, on which sun and time had now passed. Waden looked, for a moment surprised: the stone face had changed, acquired the smallest hint of a more somber look to come.

"It's different, isn't it?" Waden asked. The change was small and to the unfamiliar eye, deceptive. "It's *different*."

"It changes every moment that the sun touches it, with every season, every hour, with storm and morning and night-fall and every difference of the light . . . it changes. Yes."

Waden looked at it again, and at him, and reached and pressed his shoulder, standing beside him. "I chose you well. I chose you well, Artist."

"A matter of dispute, who chose whom. I don't grant you that point."

"But how do I see it? How does anyone see it, in its entirety?"

Herrin smiled. "It's for the city, First Citizen; for everyone who walks here and passes through it for years upon years, at varied hours in different seasons of his life, and for every person, different because of the schedule he keeps; different vision for anyone who cares to stand here for hours watching the changes progress. You're a moving target, Waden Jenks, a subject that won't hold still, and not the same to any two people. It's time itself I've sculpted into it, and the sun and the planet cooperate. Done in one season . . . it had to be. It's unique, Waden Jenks."

Waden had not ceased to look at the face, which grew steadily more sober, the illusion of light within it in the process of dying now. And the living face began to take on anxiety. "What does it become? What are the changes going toward?"

"Come at another hour and see."

"I ask you, Artist. What does it become?"

"You've seen the Apollo; Dionysus is coming. It achieves that this afternoon."

"This thing could become an obsession; I'd have to sit hour after hour to know this thing in all its shapes."

"And, I suspect, season after season. Look at the time and the sun and the quality of the light, and wonder, First Citizen, what this face is. You don't live only in the Residency any more: you're here. In this form, in changing forms."

"Would I *like* all the faces?"

Herrin smiled guardedly. "No. In Dionysus . . . are moments you might not like. I've sculpted possibilities, First Citizen, potential as well as truth. Come and see."

Waden stared at him, and said nothing.

"Whatever you see in it," Herrin said, "will change."

"I'm impressed with your talent," Waden said. "I accept the gift, in both its faces."

"No gift, First Citizen. You traded to get this, and you were right: it will give you duration. It's going to live; and when later ages think of the beginnings of Freedom, there'll be one image to dominate it. This. All it has to do is survive, and all you have to do is protect it."

Waden sucked at his lips, as he had the habit of doing when pondering something. "Now time is my worry, is it?"

"It always was; it's your deadliest enemy."

The sober look stayed, and yielded to one of Waden's quizzical smiles. "And your ally?"

"My medium," Herrin said, and for a moment Waden's smile utterly froze.

"We remain," said Waden then, recovering the smile in all its brilliance, "complementary."

There was Keye, frowning; and the invisibles, who stood with their hands tucked into their belts looking at the place and at the crowd, and the crew, who watched them. On the fringes of the crowd were the pair no one else might see, midnight-hued and tall and robed, skeletons at the feast— Herrin imagined wise and unhuman eyes, baffled—and Waden's Outsiders watching them.

People did not make crowds in Kierkegaard; citizens were rational, cautious and conservative of their own Reality, avoided masses in which they could lose their own Selves. People gathered *here,* in this shell. And suddenly, when he looked at them in general and Waden did they began a polite applause, as people might, to express approval of something they had accepted as real and true—something they desired.

Strangers applauded, and the sound went up into the triple perforated dome, and echoed down again like rain. "Herrin . . ." he heard amid it, *"Herrin," "Herrin Law,"* as if his name had become their possession too. *"Master Herrin Law."*

He smiled, sucked in the air as if sipping wine and nodded his head in appreciation of the offering. More, he spread his arms, seeing some of his chief apprentices near at hand, and invited them. "Carl Gytha," he said, "Andrew Phelps. . . ," He went on naming names, and the gathering applauded and faces grinned in pleasure. "Were you one of them?" people asked each other, and when one claimed to be, those standing next would all ask his name and touch him. Theirs were names written in bronze; names to last . . . and it was the only art which had come out of the cloistered University into the streets of Kierkegaard.

"It's unprecedented," said Keye, gazing with analytical eye on the chaos.

"Of course it is," said Herrin.

Waden laughed and squeezed his shoulder. "*You* are unprecedented, Artist; *now* it's unveiled, not before. That's the nature of your art, isn't it? It's not stone you shape—time, yes, and Realities. You're dangerous, Artist. I always knew you were."

"Complementary powers, Waden Jenks." He lifted his arm toward the face, which had lost its inner glow, which began to shadow with doubt, which led toward the other shadows of itself. "*That* . . . will be with generations to come. The weak will emulate it; the strong will be obsessed by it—because it challenges them. You'll always be there. *Give me substance*, you asked, and there you stand."

"I chose you well. Dispute what you will, I chose you well." Waden grinned like a child, pulled him round and embraced him in public, to the applause of all the crowd; and the doorways were jammed with more people seeking to know what happened there. "Walk back with me, to the Residency. They'll give you no rest here; walk back with us and let's celebrate this thing."

Herrin hesistated; he had planned to stay, or to do something else; to talk to Gytha and Phelps, he supposed, but the crowd overwhelmed him. He nodded, agreeing, and walked with Waden, with Keye, with the escort of invisibles who suddenly organized themselves to stay with them.

At the first wall of the dome, Waden stopped and looked back, with awed reluctance, but Keye watched him, and Herrin watched him and Keye.

Then they parted the crowd and headed back the way they had come, changed, Herrin thought, as everyone who came inside that place must be changed.

No one followed them—no one would dare—but the invisibles stayed at their heels, silent as they had been from the beginning.

XX

Student: How does a person fit death into his reality, sir?

Master Law: Whose?

Student: How do you fit your own death into yours, sir?

Master Law: One has nothing to do with another.

Student: You deny the reality of death?

Master Law: (After reflection.) With all my reality.

It was a pleasant day, Waden in high spirits and prone to argue. "I find myself too tired for fine discussion," Herrin confessed.

"You've grown thin," Waden said. They sat at a table in Waden's rooms in the Residency, with exquisite tableware, Waden's ordinary set . . . "*Eat* something, Herrin; you'll waste away."

"By my standards I have." Herrin leaned back, drinking tea and comfortable with a full belly. "A supper last night, a lunch today . . . gluttony. I plan to increase my tolerance."

"You have to," said Keye, third in their threesome at table. "I know your habits, Herrin, and they're abominable."

He grinned pleasantly and briefly. "I fear the Residency is responsible. I find myself reluctant to bestir the whole array of kitchens and servants. It's easier in the University to go downstairs and trouble cook for sandwiches. I'll be leaving for awhile."

Waden shrugged. "Wherever you're comfortable."

"You'll have new projects," said Keye.

He shrugged.

"What do you propose?" Waden asked.

He smiled. "I'll know when I find it."

"Ah, then you don't know."

"I suspect that I know but that it hasn't surfaced. Allow me my methods."

"You . . . have no interest in exterior events?"

"What, yours?"

"Exterior events."

"*Are* there any?"

"Rhetorical question?"

"No. Inform me. What's happening with your Outsiders? Anything of interest?"

Waden shrugged and toyed with the handle of his cup, lips pursed. He looked up suddenly. "The station module is due to arrive. Past that point it begins to grow, a station, widening of the port. . . ."

"Irrevocably."

"*My* art, Herrin. Trust that I know what I'm doing."

Herrin smiled tautly.

"Ah," said Waden Jenks. "I see the thought passing. You say nothing; ergo you have very much to say. It's only on trivialities that you debate motivation. You think—using that creation out in the Square, to have some great part in *me*."

"I do. I'm very self-interested."

Waden smiled. "I'll never carry your argument for you. Only be sure I know what it is, even unspoken."

"I'd expect nothing less. So why should I bother? Mine's a nonverbal art form."

"Beware him," Keye said, chin on hand and smiling over her empty plate.

"Which of us?" asked Waden.

"Both of you."

"And you?" asked Herrin.

"I'm always wary," she said.

That had the feel of the old, the hungry days. Herrin laughed, set down his cup. "Surely," he said, "Waden, your appointments are waiting; and I'm due a rest. I'm going to walk off this excellent meal. And rest."

He tried. He left the upper hall of the Residency and walked downstairs, thought about going to his room and attempting a nap. He was tired enough to be very much tempted, but he also knew that the moment his head touched

the pillow, he would begin thinking about what was in the
Square or about something equally preoccupying, and he
would lie awake miserable.

He walked outside, and onto the streets, and onto Main
. . . alone this time. He stopped and looked at the crowd
which still clustered about the dome, almost lost his taste for
going there at all, ever. It gave him a sense of loss, that what
had been his private possession now belonged to everyone
and he could never get to it in private again.

The crew was dispersed . . . or if they were not, at least
they would work together no more until he could conceive of
some new idea.

But the Work had its power. It drew at him inexorably,
and he strayed slowly in that unwanted direction.

"Master Law," they whispered where he passed. There was
no anonymity.

"It's beautiful," some boy ventured to say to him, a
breathless whisper in passing on the street, in fleeing his
presence: a University Master did not converse with towns-
folk, for their sakes, for their realities' sake—because theirs
were so vulnerable; but someone interrupted that silence to
offer opinion. The boy was not the last. There were others
who called it beautiful; and some who said nothing, but just
came close to him. "My father worked on it," said a freckled
girl, as if that was supposed to mean something.

"Wait," he said, but she was embarrassed and ran away,
and he never knew whose daughter it was.

He walked inside, and even now there were a great many
people in the dome, in the outer rings. He walked into the
sunlit inner chamber, where people gathered before the
image.

It was the Dionysian face. A patch of sun fallen on the
other side and at another angle had turned it into somber
laughter, dark laughter, that expression of Waden's when he
was genuinely amused.

It went on living; it possessed the chamber with a feeling
which was, to one who knew Waden in that mood, not comfortable. Herrin deserted his own creation, and kept walking,
shivering past shadows which had come to watch the watchers, invisibles.

Leona? he thought, turning back to see, but he could not

be certain, and he kept walking, slowly, out of the dome and out of the Square, farther down Main.

People here recognized him too. The novelty of that passed and he tried simply to think in peace, disturbed and distressed that even the refuge of the streets was threatened.

On one level, he thought, he should be troubled that he could not stay there; on another, he knew why . . . that he was ready to shed that idea, to be done with it, and the persistence of it frightened him. It was Waden Jenks . . . it *was* powerful, and had to be dealt with, and now that he had created this phenomenon, he could not allow it to begin to warp *him,* and his art. Having created he had to be rid of it, erase it, get it out of his thoughts so that his mind could work.

But Waden, set in motion, was not a force easily canceled.

And what Waden did threatened him, because it came at him through his own art, and gave him no peace.

Perhaps it was the intrusion of Outsiders in Freedom which made it harder to settle himself again; an intrusion argued that events were at hand which might offer subject . . . and that bothered him, the thought that no matter what he began, something might then occur which would offer more tempting inspiration: *wait, wait,* a small voice counseled him. *Observe.*

But while he waited his mind was going to have nothing to work on, and that vacancy was acute misery; an adrenalin charge with nowhere to spend it, an ache that was physical. He could not sleep again with that vacancy in his intentions; could not; could not walk about perceiving things with his senses raw as an open wound, taking in everything about him, keeping him in the state he was in.

His course took him to the end of Main, where it became highway, and led to the Camus river. From that point he could see the river itself, which led inland and inward, back to the things he had been. He walked to the edge of it, where the highway verged it along a weed-grown bank, and the gravel thrown by wheels had made it unlovely . . . the scars of too much and too careless use; it could be better, but no one cared. He sat down there and tossed gravel in and watched the disturbance in the swift-flowing surface.

In one direction it became the Sunrise Sea, and led to the other continent of Hesse; and men were going there. Human-

ity on Freedom was spreading and discovering itself, and he
had duty there.

In the other it was safety, Camus township, and Law's Valley.

I'd like to see them, he thought of his family, and then put
it down to simple curiosity, one of those instinctual things
which had outlived the usefulness it served.

He had outgrown them. It was like the crowds back there
at the dome. Approbation was pleasant but it diverted. Probably they would applaud him back in Camus Township, but
they would no more understand him than they ever had. It
was not simply that there was no going home to what had
been: there had never been anything there in the first place
but his own desire for a little triumph, to be able to explain
what he had done to those who had been there at his beginnings.

He laughed at himself and flung an entire handful of
gravel, breaking up the surface into a cluster of pockmarks.
He created the thing he wished existed, and it did, and he
could look back on it—reckoning that his family did, at distance, perceive what he was, and that was the best they could
do. They were, after all, no better than any others, and no
less hazard: like Waden Jenks. Like Keye. He found pleasure
in the crew because the crew adored him; they in fact adored
the importance they gained through him. If they were really
anything, truly able to rival him, they would suck him in and
drink him down as readily as Waden Jenks would, given the
chance.

Power was the thing. He had Waden worried; and in
fact—in fact, he told himself—Waden ought to be worried
about him, and about Keye, who was now feeding her own
reality into Waden's ear. He comforted himself with the
thought that of all humans alive who were not about to be
taken in, Waden Jenks would not be—would in no wise let
Keye have her way with him.

Creative ethics was Keye's field; indeed creative ethics, and
Keye was busy at it. She chose Waden either because, being
political herself, she comprehended him best and rejected Art,
or because she knew Herrin Law and saw she was getting
nowhere with him.

Keye's art had to have political power to function—as

Keye saw it. *He* saw an ethic in his art which Keye had never seen.

Therefore he was greater. And sure of it.

A second handful of gravel, which startled a fish and disturbed the reality of a very small life. He smiled at the conceit. The fish knew as much of Herrin Law as most did, and it was better off that way.

He stripped some of the weeds and plaited them; his fingers were sore from the abrasive and from the work, but he could do it as dexterously as he had on the grassy hillside overlooking his home.

His own bed would be a comfort, porridge cooking when he got up, the scrape of wooden chairs on wooden floor and the smells of everyone and everything he knew woven together and harmonious like the braid of grass.

Herrin, his mother would say, *time to get up. Did you hear?* his father would say. *He can go on and sleep*; that would be Perrin. *I get his bowl.*

He smiled, laughed a breath and stared into the water.

Trucks passed in one direction and the other, never slowed, but roared past on their own business; it was not the day for either bus, which wandered opposite directions of a loop somewhere in the outermost reaches of the Camus valley, linking village to village and all with Kierkegaard.

The river came from the high valleys, from places he had known. It was, even with the truck traffic, a pleasant place to sit.

It was the cold that moved him finally, the shift of wind which accompanied a line of clouds marching on the city, which ruffled the water and bent the weeds and persuaded him it was time to walk back. The sun was sinking. He thought of the dome, where the disquieting image would have settled toward peace. He wanted to see it, but he was drained, and it was cold, and he wanted only to go unrecognized and to stay private in his thoughts. He had achieved at least a measure of tranquility, and found he ached in his bones and that his feet and backside were cold.

He angled off toward the east, avoiding the straight of Main and Jenks Square. It happened to be the direction of the port, and his palate remembered meat pies. There, in the gathering twilight, existed a place where he could walk unre-

marked. All the way to the port's south gateway he thought
of the pies and the strange and peaceful market.

But there was a silence when he had gotten to the wire
fence and the open south gate. It was almost dark; he stood
there bewildered, staring at the closed booths and wondering
if he had lost track of things. He walked where there had
been the smell of things good to eat and the busy commerce
of invisibles . . . and there was nothing. There were occasional invisibles, robed forms which melded with the shadows
and the booths and the dark, between the shops and the
fence, but it was all dead; the few shapes which moved here
were like insects over the corpse of the life which had existed
here.

The port itself . . . lived. He looked out where a machine
sat in the port, stranger than any he had ever seen, a gray
monster attempting nonchalance on the soil of Freedom,
where lights glared and motors whined. It was gulping down
supply drums; and those drums were about to be lifted off
Freedom, to something which, if he looked up, would not be
visible, the size and the nature of which he did not clearly
picture to himself, although he had seen pictures of ships.

Waden's. All of this belonged to Waden, and indirectly,
therefore, to him, and yet he had never imagined it, or *had*,
in the sense that he had conceived at least of the possibility in
comprehending Waden Jenks, in that statue in Jenks Square.
Like the sculpture in the Square, it took on independent life,
surprising him, disquieting him.

His mind flinched back to the escort which had come with
Waden, the unwelcome visitants who had walked within the
dome at Jenks Square. More of them would come. His Work
was great, and all those who came to Freedom's station and
to Freedom itself would be drawn to it. He thought of
Camden McWilliams and the Pirela weavings, and felt a
slight insecurity, the apprehension of a destructive, not a
creative, force, which had begun to disturb him even then.
He remembered the face and the form which were safely shut
in that sketchbook he had not touched after that day, that
dark and overlarge figure which had occupied Waden Jenks's
office as that ship occupied the port, radiating things Outside,
a figment of Waden Jenks's private ambitions, which now began to have many faces.

That was what had begun to nag at him, that was the dis-

turbance which had made these strangers unbearable to him
. . . that unfinished portrait and the whole concept behind it,
that . . . presence . . . in the untouched sketchbook, which
was not a part of Freedom's reality, and was; and was his;
and was not. It was in there, imprisoned in the leaves, reminding him of the same thing the machine out there told
him—that within the ambition of Waden Jenks, and therefore
within his own, was the like of Camden McWilliams and the
foreign colonel who wanted him . . . what, dead? Was that
what became of enemies in the Outside? It was all full of un-
certainties, things half-formed.

That was what kept at him. *Open the book,* it said, that
unfinished sketch, wanting him to do something with it, interpret it, bring it the rest of the way into view of all the rest of
these people, for Waden and for Keye and for the city, make
them see what he saw, make their vision . . .

. . . Outward.

As his kept leading him. *Look,* look at the potential in this
individual; consider the perspective of his being; look at the
hazard; and the possibility; look.

See him, this invisible, this Outsider.

He wiped his mouth, which had gone dry, stared at the inspiration which was trying, combined with what sat out there
in the floodlights, to rear up inside him and claim his undivid-
ed attention.

His own reality suddenly discarded the whole project of
the expedition to Hesse as irrelevant—an expedition to a
place which would be as rude and bare of need for art as
Law's Valley; the prospect stifled him. This, on the other
hand, *this* argued for seizing an opportunity before Waden
Jenks could have it all his way, before Keye could work upon
Waden or anyone else. Make them see *his* visions instead. . . .

Camden McWilliams. Waden had betrayed the man to his
hunters, had traded that man and that information for what
Waden wanted, which was the station Freedom had never
had since the colony ship broke up. A second chance. And
from that second chance, that station which would bring the
military to Freedom—a chance to extend the grasp of Waden
Jenks. To take the minds of their leaders, to divert them for
his purposes . . . all these things.

Camden McWilliams, whatever else he was and whatever

potential he had, became the commodity in this trade, which was being made now, for good or for ill for Freedom. That brooding black figure stayed central in his thoughts, the solitary image, dark, like the Outside; unknown, like the Outside.

He started walking, toward the University, toward the studio. The port, the street, the stairs passed in a blur of other thoughts, of visions which began like fevered dreams to tumble one over the other. He forgot about supper, remembered it when he was already in the University building, and from one direction there was a soft noise of the Fellows' Hall, and in the other the stairs, and the studio.

He had no appetite for food now, not with the other hunger.

He took the stairs, the way to the studio which he had visited only infrequently of late. He walked into the studio and turned on the light. Everything was disordered as he had left it, dusty with neglect. He kicked papers this way and that, kicked some old rags aside—they were for wiping his hands from the clay. He remembered where he had left the sketchbook on the table by the bed, sat down on the rumpled sheets—no servants ever gained access here; they had never been permitted. He knew the place and the page, and opened it to that series dark with shading out of which the Outsider face stared. He had caught the expressions, the frowns, the menace, the poses of the powerful body. It was all there; he remembered.

He laid the book down and made the pages stay open, cleared a working surface on the second of the modeling tables—the first one still held models for the dome—and opened the vat by the tableside, scooped out large handfuls of wet clay, flung them onto the surface, lidded the vat and straightened, his hands already at it. He should stop, should change to his working garments—there was already clay on his black clothes—but the vision was there, now. He worked, feverish in his application, blinded by what he saw it should become if he could only get it in time.

It became. He watched it happen and loathed what he was creating, but it went on becoming, a face, features contracted as if it stared into something unapprehended, a force, which itself radiated and got nothing back. There was despair within it; there was—hate. It was citizen Harfeld's look, and his sister Perrin's; it was that of Leona Pace, that hunger which never filled itself, which stared at lost things and never-had things and ached and got nothing back.

XXI

Waden Jenks: You've taught me something.
Master Law: What, I?
Waden Jenks: That duration itself is worth the risk; and that's my choice as well, Artist.

He stopped, when his shoulders had stiffened and his arms ached from the extension and his hands hurt from working the clay. He looked at it; he had not the strength to work to completion at one sitting. That would take days and months to do as he had done the other, but the concept wanted out of him, refusing patience, promising months of effort if he lacked the stamina to go on now, in hours, to finish what vision he had. It sat rough and half-born, the essence of it there. He touched the wet clay, brushed at it tentatively and finally surrendered, dropped his hand and folded his arms on the table and rested his head on them and slept where he sat, fitfully, until he gained the strength to walk over and fall into the unmade bed——to waken finally with hands and arms painfully dry and caked thick with clay, to open his eyes and stare across the room at the creature on the table as if it were some new lover that had come into the room last night and stayed for morning. He had feared it was a dream which might fade out of reach; but it was there, and demanded, unfinished as it was, an attention he presently could not give it.

He washed, stiff-muscled and shivering in the unheated studio; dressed, because he had not taken all his clothes away to the Residency, against some time that he would want this place. He paused time and time again to stare at what he had done in the fit of last night, and it no more let him go than

before, except that he had spent all his vision and was
drained for the time. He knew better than to lay hands on it
now, when nothing would come out true, when his hands and
his eye would betray him and warp what he remembered.
The vision was retreated into the distance and hands alone
could not produce it or impatience force it. It was waiting. It
would come back and gather force and break out in him
again when he had rested. He had only to think about it and
wait.

Never—he was sure—never exactly as it had been last
night; those impulses, once faded, could not be recovered. He
mourned over that, and paused in his intention to go downstairs to breakfast, just to look toward that disturbing face.

He laughed then at his own doubt. It had more in it than
the work he had just finished, more of potential. It could be
greater than what was in Jenks Square. It could become . . .
far greater. He suffered another impulse to work on it, which
was not an impulse he ought to follow. After breakfast; after
rest; then.

People approached the door; classes were starting, he reckoned. It was daybreak; maybe someone was starting early.

The door opened. It was Waden.

"Well," Herrin said, because Waden's visits to University
were normally limited to the dining hall. Outsiders were with
him. Evidently that was going to be a permanent attachment.
"*I* was headed downstairs."

"You've been working." Waden walked to the table,
touched the clay, walked around it. Frowned and touched it
again. "That's what you're doing next."

"It's far from finished."

"McWilliams. He's not like that. He's a narrow, narrow
man. You make him a god."

"I've only borrowed his features. It's not McWilliams; just
the shell of him."

"This is *good*."

"Of course it is."

"Did you have this in mind all along?"

"Started it last night. . . . Do you have a point, Waden?
Come down to breakfast with me."

"I don't want you to do any more statues."

Herrin stood still and looked at him. "Am I to take you
seriously?"

"Absolutely."

"First Citizen, you're given to bizarre humor, but this—whatever it demonstrates—is not for discussion at breakfast."

"It has rational explanation, Herrin. I'm sure you even understand it."

He thought about it. The best thing to do, he thought, was to walk out the door on the spot and give Waden's absurdity the treatment it deserved; but the doorway was occupied: invisibles stood there, Waden's escort, large men with foreign weapons. And he did see them and Waden knew that he saw them.

"You were useful," Waden said, "in creating what you did. Art's the more valuable while it's unique. If you go on creating such things, you'll eventually overshadow it. I'm telling you . . . there'll not be another. You've created something unique. *Protect it,* you said; *time is your enemy,* you said; and I believe you, Herrin."

He was cold inside and out. It was very difficult to relax and laugh, but he did so. "I recall what your art is; but do you fancy years of Keye alone? You need me more than ever, First Citizen. Look at your allies and imagine dialogue with them."

"I know," Waden said. "I agree with you on all of that. I don't want to lose you. You've accomplished a great deal. You're a powerful force; you've swallowed up Kierkegaard itself; you have people doing strange things and Kierkegaard will never be the same. But, Herrin, you've done as much as I want you to do. As much as I *want* you to do. Enjoy everything you have. Bask in your success. *Know* that you've warped a great many things about your influence, and that you'll have your duration. *Look,* they'll say for ages to come, *look* at the work of Herrin Law; he only made one, and laid down his tools and stopped, because it was a masterwork, and it was perfect. Quit while your reputation is whole. Stop at this apex of your career, and you'll challenge ages to come with what you've done; you'll have accomplished everything you ever said you wanted. *Paint,* if it suits you. Painting's not the same kind of art; your sketches are brilliant. Be rich. Teach others. Continue here as a Master. Do anything in the world you like. You want comfort—have it. You want influence—I'll give you control of the whole University. Just don't do another sculpture."

"At your asking."

"I ask this," Waden said quietly, "I *plead* with you—which I have never done with anyone and never shall again."

"Meaning that you're threatened; meaning that my art has to give way to yours, and you mean I should admit that."

"Mine is the more important, Herrin. My art guides and governs, but yours is Dionysian and dangerous. It provokes emotion; it gathers irrational responses about it; it touches and it moves, like energy itself. While your energy serves me I use it, but you've done enough. It's time to stop, Herrin, because if you go further you put yourself in conflict with me. You threaten order. And you threaten other things. I asked you to lend me duration; and now I have to be sure you don't lend it to anyone else. Like that—" He gestured toward the sculpture. "*That*, a man hunted by agencies friendly to us—"

"Your reality's becoming bent indeed if you care in the least what *they* think. If you had power you'd tell them what to think. But aren't you losing your grip on it—that the best you can do is come here and tell me *not* to create, that your reality can't withstand me and what I do? Are you that fragile, Waden Jenks? I never thought so until now."

"You misunderstand. The power is not illusory. It is *real*, Artist, and it can be used. I've told you what I want and don't want, and the fact that I can tell you is at issue here, do you see that? All you have to do is admit that I can. And think about it. And take the rational course. Leave off making statues. That's all I ask."

Herrin shook his head. "Really an excellent piece of your art, Waden. Consummate skill. I *am* intimidated. But I exist, I do what I do, and it's not to be changed."

"I understand. You won't give in, reckoning this is a bluff, that at any moment I'll let you know you've been taken." Waden reached to the table beside him, took up dried clay in his fingers and crumbled it. Suddenly he grasped the table edge and upended it.

Herrin exclaimed in shock and grabbed for it; but it fell; the head hit the floor and distorted itself and he grabbed for Waden, seized up a handful of impeccable suit and headed Waden for the wall.

The Outsiders grabbed him from behind, hauled him back

while he was still too shocked at the touch itself; and at the destruction; and at Waden Jenks.

"I'm very serious," Waden said. "Believe me that you *won't* go on working as you please, and I know what it is to you—admit it, admit that after all, you don't control what happens, and ask me, just ask me for what I've offered you, on my terms . . . because those are the terms you'll get. Those are the terms you have to live with. It's my world. I can make it comfortable for you—or harsh; and all you have to do to save yourself a great deal of grief is to admit that truth, and follow orders, which is all you've ever really done. Only now you have to see it and to deal with that fact. Admit it. When you can—you're quite safe."

"I'm not about to." Herrin tried to shake himself loose. It was going to take losing the rest of his composure and still he entertained the suspicion it was all farce. "We'll talk about this later. Rationally."

"No. There's no talk left. I just ask you whether you're willing to be reasonable in this. That's all."

"Oh, well, I agree."

"You're lying of course, I know. Humor me, you think, try eventually to move me. No. I'm leaving now, Herrin. I've borrowed these troops from the port; they don't have the reluctance in some regards anyone else in Kierkegaard would have. Others wouldn't lay a hand on you, but they will. They'll see to it that you can't use that talent of yours again. You see, I also deal with the material as well as the mind; and by the material—on the mind. I don't want him killed— understand me well—I just want it assured he won't make any more statues. Physically. Herrin, I don't want it this way."

"Then you've already lost control."

"It's not a game, Herrin; not a debate: I'm leaving. And if you ask me and I know you've come to my Reality, Herrin, you can get out of this." Waden walked to the door, waited, looked back. "Herrin?"

He shook his head, suddenly made up his mind and jerked loose, headed for Waden in the intent of getting to him, the head, the center of it; a hand grasped his arm, dragging at him and he spun, elbowed for a belly and rammed his free hand for a throat, but they hauled at his arms again. There was no one in the doorway; the door closed, in fact leaving him with them, and a blow slammed into his midsection in the instant he looked.

He threw his whole body into it, rammed his feet into one of them, twisted with manic force and threw one of them over, came down on that one and rammed a freed forearm into his face. A blow dazed him, sent his vision red and black, and he tried to heave himself for his feet, met a body and heaved his weight into it. The body and a table went over, and they went on hitting him, over and over again, until his balance left him and he hit the floor on hip and shoulder. "Don't kill him," one reminded the others. "Don't risk killing him." One trod on his arm, and a boot came down on his hand, smashed down on it repeatedly. He tried to protect himself, but they had him, rolled him on his face and smashed the other hand. He had not, to his knowledge, made a sound—did then, cried out from the pain and lost all his organization to resist the blows that came at him and the blurred figures which swarmed over him. He curled up when they had let him go. Even that instinctual move came hard, muscles twitching without coordination, some paralyzed. One of them kicked him in the belly and he could not prevent it.

They walked away then. He lay aching on the concrete floor and heard the door open and close. He moved his arms and tried to move his legs and to lift his head. His stomach started heaving, dry heaves that racked torn muscles from chest to groin. He tried to push his right hand against the floor and there was both pain and numbness. He saw the hand in front of him distorted beyond human form, hauled the left arm from under his ribs and went sick with the pain as wrist and fingers ground under him, that hand distorted like the other. He moaned to himself, tried again and again to roll onto his elbow to get an arm under him while his stomach spasmed. He collapsed, tried it again, finally sat up and tucked his wounded hands under his arms, rocking and grimacing against the pain that washed over him in blurring waves.

He saw himself finally. He saw himself sitting in a room where enemies could come back and find him, to hurt him further or simply to stare. He saw himself faced with the need to go outside, a Master of the University, who had to go maimed into public view and face the people who had feared him and the people who had relied on him for their own realities, and the students he had taught and most of all Waden Jenks and Keye Lynn. He shuddered, swallowed down another spasm and could not stop shivering. He tried to get up, finally made it, still doubled over, and reached the wall to lean on.

Had to go out. There was nowhere to go and nowhere to stay. He hurt, and he could not straighten, could not even change the clothes which were smeared with clay and dust and blood. He tried, ineffectually, to straighten the studio . . . gathered up the sketchbook which had been stepped on, clenching his teeth against the waves of sickness. Tried. There was no saving the clay; it was ruined, and he did not want to look at it. He managed finally to stand with his back against the wall, though it hurt, managed to catch his breath.

Waden's reality. They came now, the Outsiders, whenever they would; and wherever they would . . . Waden's doing. Waden had meant this—always meant this.

His eyes stung; he wept, and pushed from the wall to the doorway, managed finally with his ruined hand to reach the latch and to open it.

No one saw him, down the hall and down the stairs. They looked at first, but he flinched and they flinched from seeing him.

He fell on the steps outside. It was a moment before he could recover from the impact, and some had started toward him, but when he looked up at them and they looked at him, they pretended they had been going somewhere else, because he had fallen from more than the height of the steps, and he knew it and they knew it. It was a matter outside their realities. He gathered himself up finally, and leaned against the wall for a time until he could walk.

He did so, then, because he ached and walking seemed to make the ache less, or it distracted him, or it was the only reality he had left, simple motion to evidence life. He was no longer sure.

XXII

Waden Jenks: Freedom is my beginning, not my limit.
Master Law: We once talked of hubris.
Waden Jenks: And discounted it.

He kept walking, a slow, a public process . . . incredible
how long it took just to go the length of the building unsup-
ported; or to try the next distance. He went the opposite way
from the Residency, which was along Port Street, and necessarily toward the port, because there was no way off Port
Street in this direction but that wire gate at the end. There
were some students walking, three, four meetings to endure;
but they passed without evidencing that they saw. He walked
bent, because of the pain, and when he would reach a place
where there was a surface to lean on he would rest. He was
not, at present, rational, and knew it, but standing still hurt,
and he was too ashamed to sit down. He had no idea where
he was going, only where he refused to go, which was to
Waden Jenks, or to the center of Kierkegaard where people
could see him, or the University where he had to face people
he had taught and people he had directed.

The port gateway was ahead; he did not want that either,
but when he stopped, swaying on his feet and subconsciously
reckoning how long he could stand without falling and how
much strength he had . . . he conceived of himself wander-
ing mindlessly back and forth, back and forth on Port Street
between the Residency and the University until he dropped,
too dazed to do otherwise.

He went for the port. Passed the vacant gateway, walked
along the edge by the fence, leaning on it when he had to,
shoulder against the wooden posts and wire, scuffling through
the debris the wind gathered there, among the empty drums
and stacked cargo bins. The stacks were the only privacy he

had found. He dropped to his knees and leaned against the wire and curled up, trying to will the pain away, winced from the sight of his hands, which were knotted and swollen, at once so deadened and so bone-deep with pain that he could not let them hang down. He kept them tucked up, so that the blood did not throb in them so much. He rocked because motion comforted, even when he lacked the strength to walk.

It got worse. And worse. The numbness of the injuries wore off, and he sat still finally, in a haze of pain; the only comfort was the chill of the concrete and he stretched out on it three quarters on his face, simply trying to last through it.

He was thirsty; that, most of all. His lips were cracked and his tongue stuck to his mouth. He thought of places he could get a drink, one by one realized they involved witnesses. There was the river itself if he could walk that far, but he could not, at present. Once there had been the port market, but he was not sure it was open; what had been going on out here at the port, what had been going on in general, he had no clear picture because until now he had not wanted to know. He wished he could think. He was, he knew on one level, functioning on animal instinct; and it was keeping him going when perhaps he was going to wake up from this and wish he had not survived it. He had no idea what else to do but what he had done.

Waden perhaps expected him to come back, to plead for shelter; he reckoned that he could still do that. A sting of anger welled up in his eyes, but he had no tears. Keye . . . was with Waden. And there was no one else. Shivers began, convulsive and painful, which jerked muscles against damaged joints, and for a long time he lay as still as he could with as little thought as he could, only counting the intervals and trying to calculate whether the spasms were increasing or decreasing.

After that came a blur of time and misery. He heard machinery, once jolted awake in the apprehension that the moving of drums might crush him, because the booming and shifting of the loaders came nearer and nearer. Then it stopped, and there was nothing for a long time, but cold. The sky clouded, and the warmth of the sun diminished, even that. He laughed at that final calamity, in which the whole universe conspired.

And he wept.

Finally, because a feverish strength had come back to him, and because the paving itself had begun to hurt his joints, he worked at getting to his feet again. Walked, following the fence which divided the port from Kierkegaard. Far across the pavement, diminished by distance, the alien machines conducted their business; and somewhere across the port, Outsiders settled into residence behind new fences. He saw the market, a scattering of small buildings and stalls, and his pulse quickened with hope, because some looked open, at least a few of them. He staggered in that direction, tried to straighten and walk normally, but he could not keep his steps from weaving.

Outsiders were among the shoppers, trading among the booths, strangers in no-color uniform; and citizens staunchly pretended not to see them while they were robbed of whatever the Outsiders wanted to carry off.

"*Look* at them," Herrin raged when an Outsider simply walked away from a merchant with a silver bracelet. "*See* them; they're *here*." But no one did; no one seemed to see him, standing out from the market on the pavement, filthy and disheveled. Only some of the Outsiders looked his way, and he went cold under those stares, hesitating to come in at all until they had decided to go about their business.

There were booths where food was sold, and drink; Outsiders clustered there, and some owners must have left, because some booths were wholly Outsider, with an Outsider tending grill and tapping the beer and passing it out as fast as it could come.

Citizens crowded together at one booth . . . where a harried woman tried to keep up with demand, where mugs were snatched as soon as they could be poured, and Herrin thrust his way into the crowd which melted about him, tried to get to his pocket where he had a little money, but his hands could not bear the pain. "I have money," he said to the woman at the counter. "I *have* money," because he was not an invisible, who could pilfer what he wanted. "If someone could get it from my pocket. . . ." But she paid no attention to him, just mopped at the crumbs on the counter and took an order from someone else. She set the mug on the counter, amber and frothing and wet, and he reached for it in desperation, with a hand that could not hold it; the owner did not stop him. "I want my beer!" the man shouted at the owner as if she had failed to deliver his order; and Herrin got his other arm to the counter, braced the mug between his wrists and got it to his lips. The cold liquid eased his mouth and throat. He found space about him; the crowd had simply melted aside and come at the booth from another angle, while he stood hunched and drinking with huge, bitter swallows, all the while feeling the heavy wet glass sliding from his awkward grip on it.

"Master Law," a female voice said, and someone touched him gently on the arm. He looked round into Leona Pace's eyes, a face surrounded by chestnut hair and a blue hood.

"Get away from me!" He dropped the mug, and it broke. He lurched away and stumbled, recovered and kept going. She did not follow. He fled, until he came to the corner of a building and leaned there, and suddenly found himself face to face with Outsiders.

He turned and ran, darted into another aisle, bent with pain and uncontrolled. Walkers evaded his touch, even when he stumbled and sprawled; he lay on the concrete and they simply walked around him.

One did not. He saw blue robes sink into a puddle of cloth, felt a touch. *Leona,* he thought, willing finally to surrender, because he knew where he was, and what he had become. He levered himself up to look into the face that looked at him, and saw blue skin like leather, wet and large black eyes, a nose—if it was a nose—that curved toward something like a mouth. A hand was on his shoulder; he began to shudder as it moved to touch his back. It spread the midnight blue cloak, which smelled of wild grass and country herbs and something dry and old; it enveloped him. He stared into a face . . . nothing at all human, with that hypnotized compulsion with which he looked at a model, the liquid black of the vast eyes, at midnight blue skin which took alien, symmetrical folds about down-arching nose and pursed, small mouth. The teeth were small and square, inverted lips parted upon them as if it might speak. His arm shuddered under him and he feared falling, being helpless with this thing, whose cloak was about him. *Go away,* he almost said, and bit it back; he did not see this thing, refused to see it.

Its arm across his back tightened and it pulled him over face-up; he resisted and stopped resisting in panic. He did not see it, refused this reality; and the other arm slid beneath his legs as it gathered him to its breast beneath the cloak. Panic assailed him, fear of being dropped in his pain—no one had handled him that way, ever, in his memory; in infancy, surely, but that was not in his memory—was not *there*, and did not happen. It was strong; he had never comprehended ahnit as strong. It rose with him without apparent effort, hugged his stiff body against it the more tightly and snugged the cloak about him, enveloping him in its scent, its color, its reality. He was aware of its powerful strides, of the sound of sane citizens it passed, of conversations which passed without interruption by a reality which was not theirs.

Help me, he might cry to them; but there was nothing there when they should look, nothing that they would want to see, only something which had been Herrin Law being swept away by something which had nothing to do with humans.

There was no pity, not for what they did not perceive.

There was no fighting this thing, for even by fighting he lost. He tried not to feel what was happening, nor to perceive anything about him; he retreated into his own mind, rebuilding the reality he chose, as he chose, which ignored the pain, which denied that anything extraordinary had happened this morning, insisted that in fact he might continue to be in his bed, to sleep as late as he chose. That if he chose to open his eyes—in his imagination he did—he would see the clay bust of Camden McWilliams sitting on the table as it had been, where it would go on sitting until he chose to do something with it.

His reality, as he chose to have it.

He imagined the clay under his undamaged hands, imagined it malleable again and the face, the most perfect work he had ever done (but he would do others) gazing into infinity with a look of desire.

He felt the arms about him. He had gone limp within them, yielded to the motion; it had nestled him more comfortably, and there was dark cloth between him and the daylight, a woven fabric which scarcely admitted the declining sun; there was alien perfume in his nostrils; there was midnight cloth against his cheek, which rested on a bony breast as hard as the arms which enfolded him.

No, he thought to himself, trying to rebuild that warm bed in the studio. When he was aware, his hands hurt, and his ribs did, and the pain throbbed in rhythm with his heart and the movement of what carried him. He made no move. Horror occurred to him, that perhaps it took him away to commit some further pain on him, or to feed on . . . he knew nothing of ahnit, or what they did, and there was no rationality between human and ahnit.

There is no relevancy, he insisted to himself. It and Herrin Law were not co-relevant; and what it in its reality chanced to do to Herrin Law were overlapping but unrelated events.

He could choose not to feel it; but his self-control was frayed already by the pain. And he was not strong enough to prevent it, had not even the use of his hands.

Here was an external event; he had met one or his mind had betrayed him and conjured one. It had taken him up, and the three greatest minds on Freedom, he and Waden Jenks and Keye Lynn . . . had not planned this. Only he might have caused it. He had shaped his reality; and the shape of it suddenly argued that he had not been wise.

Or that something was more powerful, which was a possibility that undid all other assumptions.

Muscles glided, even, long steps; arms shifted him for comfort, adjusted again when the position hurt his ribs and he flinched. The pain eased and it kept walking. He heard nothing more of the human voices of the port, heard rather the whisper of grass, and his heart beat the harder for realizing that they had passed beyond help and hope of intervention. The pain had ebbed and exhaustion had passed and his betraying senses were threatening to stay focused, to keep him all too aware of detail he had no wish to comprehend.

It's not here, he tried to tell himself, testing the power of his mind; but sense told him that it was striding down a steep slope; that he heard water moving and smelled it . . . they had come to the river. It might fall, or might drop him, or even fling him in, and he could not catch himself. His hands throbbed, shot pain through his marrow—it shifted its grip, was going to drop him. . . .

He stiffened and slipped, tried to catch at its shoulder and could not, his hand paralyzed; but it caught him itself and slowly, a shadow between him and the sinking sun, its cloak still tenting him, eased him to the ground. He hurled his body frantically aside, to get away, but it knelt astride him and pressed his shoulder down, keeping him from going anywhere. He twisted his head. They were beside the water, on the riverbank. He looked dazedly at the brown current, staring in that direction and trying to think, muddled with pain and longing for the water; he had hurt his hand trying to use it. The pain was starting up again, headed for misery.

The ahnit got off him, a tentative release; he stayed still, not looking at it, reasoning that if he treated it as humans always did, it might treat him as ahnit always did and simply go away.

It moved into his unfocused vision, a mere shadow, and dipped water; it *was* only a shadow—he had achieved that much. But then the shadow moved closer and obscured all his view, like dark haze in the twilight; it leaned above him and laid a cold wet hand on his brow, so that he flinched. It bathed his face with light touches of leathery thin fingers. It leaned aside and dipped up more water and repeated the process. *Let it*, Herrin thought, and tried to stare through it.

Then it picked up his hand, and he flinched and cried out from the pain. It did not let go, but eased its grip. He stared into the midnight face, the wet dark eyes. Tried, with tiny movements, to indicate he wanted to pull his hand back; even that hurt.

"You see me," it said.

It was a rumbling, nasal voice. A rock might have spoken. It chilled him and he ceased even to reason; he jerked from it and hurt himself. Quickly it let him go.

"You see me," it said again.

He stared at it, unable to unfocus it. It reached to his collar, touched the brooch he wore there, forgotten. "You see this, you see me."

And when he had almost succeeded in unfocusing again, it unpinned the brooch that he had handled daily, that he had worn in defiance of others, thinking it a vast joke. It was no-color, like the ahnit.

"See it," said the ahnit, "see me."

He could not deny it.

"I have a name," said the ahnit. "Ask it."

"I see you," he said. It was hard to say. It was suicide. He gave up hope. The ahnit uncloaked itself, unclasping the brooch at its own throat, and baring an elongate, naked head, and a robed body which hinted at unhuman structure; it spread the cloak over him, bestowing oblivion, spreading warmth over his chilled body.

"Go away," he asked it.

It stayed, a shadow in the almost dark, solid, undeniable.

"Do they all begin this way?" he asked of it.

"They?" it echoed.

"All the others who see you."

"No others."

"Leona Pace."

"They don't see. They look *at* us, but they don't see."

It had the flavor of proposition. Like a Master, it riddled him and waited response, conscious or unconscious of the irony. He searched his reason for the next Statement and suddenly found one. "My reality and yours have no meaning for each other."

"They talk about reality. They say they lose theirs and they're no longer sane."

"They obviously talk to you."

"A few words. Then no more. They try to go back; and they live between us and you. They just talk to themselves."

"From that you know how to talk to us."

"Ah. But we've *listened* for years."

"Among us." The prospect chilled. No one had known the ahnit *could* speak; or wanted to know; or cared. Humans chattered on; and ahnit—invisible—listened, going everywhere, because no one could see them. He shook his head, trying to do what the others had done, retreating to a safer oblivion; but he had been in the port, had tried to function as an invisible, and it had not saved him from shame.

Or from this.

"We've waited," said the ahnit.

It was Statement again. "For what?" he asked, playing the game Masters had played with him and he had played with Students in his turn. He became Student again. "For what, ahnit?"

"I don't know the word," it admitted. "I've never heard it." It made a sound, a guttural and hiss. "That's our word."

"That's *your* reality; it has nothing to do with mine."

"But you see me."

It was an answer. He turned it over in his mind, trying to get the better of it. Perhaps it was the pain that muddled him; perhaps there was no answer. He wanted it to let him go . . . *wanted* something, if the words would not have choked him on his own pride. The fact was there even if he kept it inside. Had always been there. He had denied it before. Tried to cancel it.

Truth was not cancelable, if there was something that could coerce him; and he had no wish to live in a world that was not of his making . . . in which Waden Jenks and his Outsiders, and now an ahnit limited his reach, and crippled him, and sat down in front of him to watch him suffer.

"What do you want?" he challenged it, on the chance it would reveal a dependency.

"You've done that already," it said, and destroyed his hope. "Do you want a drink, Herrin Law?"

It was not innocent. He looked into the approximate place of its eyes in the dark, in its dark face, and found his mouth dry and logic on the side of its reality; it *knew* what it did and how it answered him. He defied it and rolled onto his belly, crawled to the water's edge and used his broken hands to dip up the icy water, drank, muddying his sleeves and paining his hands, then awkwardly tried to get himself back to a dry spot, lay there with his head spinning, feeling feverish.

Patiently it tucked the cloak about him again, silent statement.

"Why did you bring me here?" he asked. Curiosity was always his enemy; he recognized that. It led him places better avoided.

"I rest here," it said.

Worse and worse places. "Where, then?"

A dark, robed arm lifted, toward the west and the hills, upriver. The road ran past those hills, but there were no farms there; were no humans there.

I'll die first, he thought, but in this and in everything he had diminished confidence. "Why?" he asked.

"Where would you go?" it asked him.

He thought, shook his head and squeezed his eyes shut, pressing out tears of frustration. He looked at it again.

"I'll take you into the hills," it said. "There are means I can find there, to heal your hurts."

An end of pain, perhaps; it worked on him with that, as Waden Jenks might, and perhaps as pitilessly. "Do what you like," he said with desperate humor. "I permit it."

The ahnit relaxed its mouth and small, square teeth glinted. "Mostly," it said, "humans are insane." Herrin's heart beat shatteringly hard when he heard that, for what it implied of realities, and this reality was devastatingly strong. "Who broke your hands, Herrin Law?"

He was trembling. "Outsiders. At Waden Jenks's orders."

"Why?"

"So there would be no more statues."

"You disturbed them, didn't you?"

He rolled his eyes to keep the burning from becoming tears, but what he saw was stars and that black distance made him smaller still. "It seems," he said, carefully controlling his voice, "that raw power has its moment."

"Where would you go?" it asked. "Where do you want to go? What is there?"

He shook his head, still refusing to blink. There was nowhere. Wherever he was, what had happened to him remained.

Carefully it slipped its arms beneath him and gathered him up, wrapped as he was in its cloak. It folded him against its bony chest and he made no resistance. It walked, and chose its own way, a sure and constant movement.

XXIII

Student: What if Others existed?
Master Law: Have they relevancy?
Student: Not to man.
Master Law: What if man were their dream?
Student: Sir?
Master Law: How would you know?
Student: (Silence.)

There was a long time that he shut his eyes and yielded to the motion, and passed more and more deeply into insensibility, jolted out of it occasionally when some stitch of pain grew sharp. Then he would twist his body to ease it, faint and febrile effort, and the ahnit would shift him in its arms, seldom so much as breaking stride. Most of all he could not bear to have his hands dangle free, with the blood swelling in them, with the least brush at the swollen skin turned to agony. He turned to keep them tucked crossed on his chest and thus secure from further hurt. He trusted the steadiness of the arms which held him and the thin legs which strode almost constantly uphill. It was all dark to him. He was lost, without orientation; the river lay behind them—there was no memory of crossing the only bridge but his memory was full of gaps and he could not remember what direction they had been facing when the ahnit had pointed toward the hills. *Across* the river, he had thought; and up the river; but then he had not remembered the bridge, and he trusted nothing that he remembered.

They climbed and the climb grew steeper and steeper. Grass whispered. The breeze would have been cold if not for the ahnit's own warmth. *We shall stop soon,* he thought, reckoning that it had him now within its own country, and that it would be content.

But it kept going, and he had time for renewed fear, that it was, after all, mad, and that he was utterly lost, not knowing back from forward. In time exhaustion claimed him again and he had another dark space.

He wakened falling, and flailed wildly, hit his hand on an arm and cried out with surprised misery. His back touched earth gently, and the ahnit's strong arms let him the rest of the way down, knelt above him to touch his face and bend above him. "Rest," it said.

He slept, and wakened with the sun in his face. Waked alone, and with nothing but grass and hills about him and a rising panic at solitude. He levered himself up, squeezing tears of pain from his eyes, broken ribs aching, and his hands . . . at every change in elevation of his head he came close to passing out. Standing up was a calculated risk. He took it, swayed on his braced legs and tried to see where he was, but there were hills in all directions.

"Ahnit!" he called out, panicked and thirsty and lost. He wandered a few steps in pain, felt a pressure in his bladder and, crippled as he was, had difficulty even attending that necessity. It frightened him, in a shamed and inexpressible way, that even the privacy of his body was threatened. His knees were shaking under him. He made it back to the place where he had slept and sank down, hands tucked upward on his chest, eyes squeezed shut in misery.

There was sun for a while, and finally a whispering in the grass. He looked toward it, vaguely apprehensive, and an ahnit came striding down the hill, cloakless. By that, it was the one which had left him here: it came to him and knelt down, regarded him with wet black eyes and small, pursed mouth, midnight-skinned. It reached beneath its robes and brought out a ball of matted grasses, contained in some inner pocket; it spread it and revealed a loathsome mass of gray-green pulp. "For your hands," it said.

He was apprehensive of it, but suffered it to take the cloak on which he sat and to shred strips from it . . . finally let it take his right hand and with its three-fingered hand—two proper fingers and opposing member—begin to spread the pungent substance over it. The touch was like ice; it comforted, numbed. "Lie down," it advised him. "Lie still. Take some of it in your mouth and you will feel less."

It offered a bit to his tongue; he took it, mouth at once numbed. In a moment more it dizzied him, and he tried to settle back. It helped him. It took his numb hand then and bound it, and while it hurt, it was a distant hurt and promised ease. "The swelling will go," it promised him. "Then I shall try to straighten the bones. And then too I will be very careful."

He drew easier breaths, drifting between here and there. It tended the other hand and probed his whole body for injury. "Ribs," he said, and with its cautious touches it exposed the bruises and salved them and bound them tightly, holding him in its arms when it had done, for the numbness had spread from his mouth to his fingertips and his toes. He breathed as well as he could, eyes shut, out of most of the pain that he had thought would never stop. Only his mouth was a misery, numb and dry; he tried to moisten his lips over and over and it seemed only worse.

It let him back then, and pillowed his head. "Rest," it seemed to whisper. He was aware of the day's warmth, of sweat trickling on him, of a lassitude too great to be borne. The sweat stopped finally, and the torment of his mouth grew worse.

"Water?" a far, alien voice asked him, rousing him enough

to focus on its dark face and liquid eyes. "I can give it from my mouth to yours if you permit."

The thought made his throat contract. He shut his eyes wearily and considered the incongruency of their mutual existence, finding their situation absurd and his fastidiousness merely a shred of the old Herrin Law, before he had begun to see invisibles and lost himself. The ahnit in his silence delicately bent to his lips, pressed his jaw open, and moisture hit the back of his throat with the faint taste of the numbing medicine. He choked and swallowed, and it let him go, letting his head back again. His stomach heaved, and the ahnit held him down with a hand on his shoulder. The spasm ceased and the pain which had shot through his ribs at the convulsion ebbed. The taste lingered. He moistened his lips and found some vague relief, suffered a flash of image, himself staring vacant-eyed at a too-bright sky because he was too drugged to care. The ahnit sat between him and the sun and shaded his face.

"It hurts less," he said thickly.

And eventually, when thirst had dried his lips again: "My mouth is dry." He did not want another such experience; but misery had its bearable limit. It leaned above him again, pressed its lips to his and this time brought up a gentle trickle that did not choke him. It drew back then, but from time to time gave him more, until he protested it was enough. It kept holding him all the same; and it spoke its own language, softly, nasals and hisses in what seemed kindly tones. He rested, finally abandoned to its gentleness, too numb to rationalize it or puzzle it, only accepting what was going to be because of what had been.

Far later in the day the ahnit took up his hand and unwrapped it. "It will hurt now," it said, and it was promising to, little prickles of feeling. The color—he focused enough to look at it—was green and livid and horrible, but the swelling was diminished. The ahnit probed it, and offered him more of the drug; he took it and settled back, trying to gather himself for the rest of it, resolved not to let the pain get through to him.

It did, and though he held out through the first tentative tug and the palpable grate of bone against bone, the subsequent splinting with knots to hold it, he moaned drunkenly on the next, and it grew worse. The ahnit ignored him, working steadily, paused when it had finished the one hand to mop the sweat from his face.

Then it started the other hand and he screamed shamelessly, sobbed and still failed to dissuade it from its work. He did not faint; it was not his good fortune. *If it were my reality,* he told himself in delirium, *I would not have it hurt.* It seemed to him grossly unfair that it did; and once: *"Waden!"* he cried out in his desperation, not knowing why he called that name, but that he was miserably, wretchedly alone. Not Keye. Waden. He sank then into a torpor in which the pain was less. He rested, occasionally disturbed by the ahnit, who held him, who from time to time gave fluid into his mouth, and kept him warm in what had begun to be night.

He was finally conscious enough to move his arm, to look at his right hand, which was swathed in fine bandage, fingers slightly curved in the splints. He was aware of the warmth of the ahnit which held his head in its robed lap, which—when he tilted his head back—rested asleep, its large eyes closed, lower lid meeting upper midway, which gave it a strange look from this nether, nightbound perspective.

The eyes opened, regarded him with wet blackness.

"I'm awake," Herrin said hoarsely, meaning from the drug.

"Does it hurt?"

"Not much."

Its paired fingers brushed his face. "Then I shall leave you a while."

He did not want it to go; he feared being left here, in the dark, but there was no reason he knew to stop it. It eased him to the ground and arranged the cloak about him, then rose and stalked away so wearily and unlike itself he could see the drain of its strength.

He lay and stared at the horizon, avoiding the sky, which made him dizzy when he looked into its starry depth; he looked toward that horizon because he judged that when the ahnit came back it would come from that direction, and he had no strength to do much else than lie where he was. All resolve had left him. Breathing itself, against the bound ribs, was a calculated effort, and the hands stopped hurting only when he found the precise angle at which he could rest them on his chest, fingers higher than his elbows. His world had gotten to that small size, only bearable on those terms.

XXIV

*Waden Jenks: Does it occur to you, Herrin, that I'm
using you?*
Master Law: Yes.
*Waden Jenks: If you were master, you wouldn't have to
argue from silences. But you must.*

He was on his feet when it returned, when the sun was just
showing its first edge, when he had decided to climb the sun-
ward slope to see what there was to see. Of what he expected
to see—the river, the city—there was no view, just more hills;
but a shadow moved, and that was the ahnit, which stopped
when it seemed to have caught sight of him, and then came
on, more wearily than before.

It said nothing to him; it simply stopped on the hillcrest
where it met him and rummaged in the folds of its robes, offered something. He started to reach for it and the pain of
moving his hand reminded him. "Food," it said, and offered a
piece to his lips. He took it, and found it to be dried and vegetable; he chewed on it while the ahnit started downslope and
he followed very carefully, aching and exhausted.

It sat down when it had gotten to the nest it had made in
the grass; it was breathing hard. When he sat down near it, it
offered another piece of vegetable to him, and he took it,
guiding it with bandaged fingers. "Better," it said to him.

"Yes," he said. The pain had been enough to fill his mind;
and then the absence of it. Now he discovered that both
states had their limit, that the mind which was Herrin Law
was going to work again; he had had his chance for oblivion
and chosen otherwise, and now—now oblivion was not so
easy. The sun was coming, and day, and he was alive because
of that same stubbornness which had robbed him of rest and
sleep in Keirkegaard . . . which, drugged, had wakened

again, incorrigible. It saw ahnit, and existed here, robbed of its body's wholeness; it just kept going, and that frightened him.

"More?" the ahnit asked, offering another piece to his lips. He used his hand entirely this time, though it hurt. "Why do you do this?" he asked the ahnit. There it was again, the curiosity which was his own worst enemy, wanting understanding which another, saner, would have fled. The ahnit, wiser, gave him no reason.

"What's your name?" he asked it finally, for it was too real not to have one.

"Sbi." It was, to his ears, hiss more than word.

"Sbi," he echoed it. "Why, Sbi?"

"Because you see me."

"Before," he said. "Sbi, did you—meet me before? Was it you?"

"I've met you before. I've been everywhere . . . in the University, in the Residency."

He shivered, hands tucked to his chest.

"Why," it asked, "are you blind to us?"

"I? I'm not. I see you very well. I'd be happier if I didn't."

"We exist," Sbi said.

"I know," he said. "I know that." It left him nothing else to know.

"Do you want water?"

He thought about it; he did, but undrugged he was too fastidious.

"It disturbs you," Sbi said.

"All right," he said, and Sbi touched his chin to steady him, leaned forward and spat just a little fluid into his mouth. Herrin shuddered at it, and swallowed that and his nausea.

"I simply store it," Sbi said, and hawked and swallowed.

"An appalling function."

"Our nature," said Sbi.

Herrin stared at Sbi bleakly. "Your reality. I'd not choose it."

Sbi made a sound which might be anything. "Mad," it said. "*Look*, at the sunrise. Can you or I make it last?"

"Material reality. *Man* counts where I'm concerned, and we can't agree."

"You've made things so complicated out of things so simple. There is the sun."

In a single flowing movement Sbi rose and walked to the hillside, stood there with hands slightly outward and face turned to the sky . . . sat down then, and ignored him entirely, seeming rapt in thoughts.

"Sbi," Herrin said finally, and Sbi looked over a shoulder at him. "What do you intend?"

"When can you walk, Master Law? I've spent too much to carry you."

"I can walk until I have to stop," he said. "A while."

"Don't harm yourself."

"What *am* I to you?"

"Something precious."

"Why?"

Sbi stood up again. "Will you walk now?"

He considered the pain of it, and nerved himself, took the cloak in his hand and used his legs more than the ribs getting up. He used his splinted hands to put the cloak to his shoulders, and Sbi helped him. The act depressed him. He bowed his head and clumsily pulled the hood up, no different finally from other invisibles; safe—no one but Sbi would see him—even in the city no one would see him. He supposed that was where they might go.

But they walked slowly, and something of directional sense, the sun being at his back, argued that they were bound only into more hills.

I shall be further lost, he thought. He did not wholly mind, because while in one sense he was dead, he was still able to see and to feel, and the mind which sometimes frightened him with its persistence of life began to yield to its besetting fault, which was at once his talent and his curse.

"You don't care," he prodded at Sbi on short breaths, "to go back to the plain. Where are you leading?"

"Where I wish."

He accepted that. It was an answer.

"See the hills," said Sbi. "Smell the wind. I do. Do not you?"

"Yes," he said. What the ahnit asked frightened him. "How much else?"

"Tell me when you know."

It took the pose of Master. His face heated, and for a little time he thought, on the knife edge of his limited breaths and the weakness of his legs in matching strides with the ahnit. "I will tell you," he said, "when I know."

He walked, with the sun beating down on him, with the gold of the grasses and the sometime gold of flowers, and it occurred to him both that it was beautiful; and that humans did not come here—ever.

He looked to the horizon, where the hills went on and on, and it occurred to him that Freedom was full of places where humans had never been.

He thought of the port, where Kierkegaard played its dangerous games with Outsiders, and Waden sought to embrace the world; there were things Waden himself did not see, choosing his own reality, in Kierkegaard, and outward.

I could make it visible, he thought, and at once remembered: *I could have. Once.*

He stopped on the next hillside, out of breath, stood there a moment. "I'm not through," he said, when Sbi offered to help him sit down.

"Rest," said Sbi. "Time is nothing."

He started walking again, hurting and stubborn, and Sbi walked with him, until he was limping and his ribs were afire. "Stop," Sbi said, this time with force, and he did so, got down, which jarred his ribs and brought tears to his eyes. He stretched out on his back, resting with his hands where they were comfortable, on his chest, and Sbi leaned over him and stroked his brow, a strange sensation and comfortingly gentle.

"Why are you blind to us?" it whispered to him.

It had asked before. "Do you play at Master?"

"Why are you blind to us?"

"Because—" he said finally, after thinking, and this time with all earnestness, "because if we shed our ways on each other . . . what becomes of us and you, Sbi? How do we choose realities?"

"I don't," said Sbi softly.

He rolled his eyes despairingly skyward and shut them because of the sun. "You don't care," he said. "Your whole existence is of only minor concern to you."

"There was a time humans saw their way to come here to Freedom; there was a time you were so wise you could do that; and there was a time you saw us, before my years. But you took your river and built your cities and stopped seeing us; you stopped seeing each other. Why are you blind to each other, Herrin Law?"

He shook his head slowly, not liking where that question led.

"Why did they cripple you?"

"Because I saw." He lost his breath and tried to get it back, with a stinging in his eyes. He felt cold all the way to the marrow. "We're wrong, aren't we, Sbi?"

"What do you think, Master Law?"

"I don't know," he said, and blinked at the sun, which could not drive the cold away. "I don't know. Where are we going, Sbi? Where are you taking me?"

"Where you'll see more than you have."

He shivered, nodded finally, accepting the threat. Sbi slid a thin arm under his shoulders and supported him as if the cold were in the air, resting with arms about him and sleeves giving him still more warmth.

And finally he found his breath easier again and knew he had strength for more traveling. "When you're ready," he said quietly to Sbi, "I am."

Sbi's three-fingered hand feathered his cheek. "Are you so anxious?"

"I won't like it, will I?"

"I might carry you a distance."

"No," he said, and began to struggle, with Sbi's careful help, to sit, and then to stand up. He was lightheaded. It took Sbi's assistance to steady him.

Perhaps, he thought, there was much of Waden in Sbi, to persuade, to create belief—to prove, at the last, and cruelly, that he was twice taken in. Perhaps Sbi also had a Talent, and perhaps Sbi was coldblooded in his waiting, since he had learned to reason with a human Master. Waden Jenks had disturbed a long stability between man and ahnit; and he had had no small part in it.

Perhaps there was a place that Sbi would turn as Waden had.

He pursued it, to know. It was all the courage he had left.

And late, after hours of sometime walking and walking again, when the sun had gotten to the west and turned shades of gold, they crossed the final hill.

He had been ready to stop. His side hurt, and tears blurred. "I'll carry you a little distance," Sbi had offered, but

he hated the thought of helplessness and kept walking, wondering deep in his muddled thoughts why of a sudden Sbi was
so anxious to keep going.

Then he passed one hill and looked on the base of another
mostly cut away; on a gold, pale figure which stood in a
niche beneath the hill. There had been no prior hint that
such existed, no prelude nor preface for it, in paths of worn
places or adjacent structure. "Is that it?" Herrin asked. "Is
that where we're going?"

"Come," said Sbi.

Herrin started downslope, and his knees threatened to give
with him and throw him into a fall he could not afford; he
hesitated, and Sbi took his arm and steadied him, descended
with him, sideways steps down the slick, dusty grass until
they were in the trough of the hills, until he could look close
at hand at the figure sculpted there, in the recess of living
stone.

It was ahnit. It was not one figure but an embrace of figures, a flowing line, a spiral . . . he moved still closer and
saw ahnit faces simplified to a line which he would never
have guessed, ideal of line and curve in a harmony his human eye would never have discovered, for it did not, as he
would have done, try to find human traits, but made them
. . . grandly other, grandly what they were. They shed tranquility, and tenderness, and, in that embrace, that spiral of
figures, the taller extended a robed arm, part of the spiral,
but beckoning the eye into that curve, in the flow of drapery
and the touch of opposing hands. It was old; on one side the
wind had blurred the details, but the feeling remained.

Herrin reached to touch it, remembered the bandages in
the motion itself, and with regret, not feeling the stone,
stroked it like a lover's skin. He looked up at alien form, at
something so beautiful, and not his, and loss swelled up in his
throat and his eyes. "Oh, Sbi," he said. "Did you have to
show me this?"

There was silence; he looked back. Sbi had joined hands
on breast and bowed, but straightened then and looked at
him, head tilted. "You made such a thing too," said Sbi. "For
all the years the city was plain and people walked without
meeting . . . but you found something else."

"I *created* something else."

"No," said Sbi. "Don't you know yet what you did? It was always there. It was always real. Your skill found it."

It offended him. He was acutely conscious of the presence above him, the alien pedestal on which he rested his hand. "So where does it exist to be found?"

Sbi folded upright hands to brow, indicating something inward, a graceful gesture.

"Then I created it," said Herrin. "It wasn't there before."

"No," said Sbi. "You only shaped the stone. You made nothing that was not before. There is one maker; but an artist only finds."

"A god, you mean. You're talking about an external event. A prime cause. You believe in that."

Sbi made a humming sound. "You believe in Herrin Law. Is that more reasonable?"

Herrin shook his head confusedly, suspecting the ahnit mocked him. And the work above him oppressed him with its power. He looked up at it, shook his head hopelessly. "Who made this?" he asked.

"Long ago," said Sbi. "Long dead. The name is lost. Few come here now, so close to your kind; the place goes untended and the grass grows. If humans came here, they couldn't see it; not minds, not eyes. But you see us."

"We share a reality," Herrin said. "That's what you saw . . . that this . . . is in common. What I made, and this."

"What you found in the stone," said Sbi. "What you found in Waden Jenks."

"I was mistaken about Waden Jenks," he said bitterly.

"Perhaps not," said Sbi.

Pain welled up in him the more strongly. He shook his head a second time and walked back from the statue, the entwined figures which beckoned his eyes into the heart of them. He made a helpless gesture, shook his head a third time, seeing things in the statue he had not seen before, the delicate work of the hands which touched, the faces which looked one almost into the other, suggesting a motion caught in intent, not completion.

"It's triangular," he said. "There should be a third. It's missing."

"No," said Sbi. "It's here."

His skin contracted. "Myself. The one who sees."

"Whoever sees," Sbi said. "You stand in the heart of them. You've become their child."

"Child." He looked at the faces, the embracing gesture, and the contraction became a shiver. They were alien. And not. "It's *good*," he said. And in despair: "I might have attained to this. Sbi, I would have. But it's better than mine. Old as it is . . . whatever it is . . . better. Before the wind got to it. . . ."

"It was a strong thought," said Sbi, "and it will take very long to fade away entirely."

"You just leave it here to be destroyed. Alone. For no one to see."

"Humans have this land now. Only a few of us remain . . . to watch. You walk past such things and don't see them; you don't see them."

"What do you see? Sbi, when you look at this, do you see things I don't?"

"Perhaps," said Sbi. "Perhaps not. We're alone in our discoveries. It's only such things as this that bind you and me together, by making us see what we thought we alone had found."

He went back, aware of the trap set up for the eye, and was drawn in all the same, into gentleness like Sbi's. He flexed at his hand and had no movement, reached out again to touch the stone, the shaping of a dead and three-fingered hand. He passed his fingers over the stone and felt very little of it but pain.

"Better than I," he said.

"At seeeing us. But looking on it has reached something in you. It *finds*, Herrin Law."

He looked aside, his knees aching and unsteady, went back to the hillside and dropped down. He absorbed the pain dully, holding his breath, settled, holding his side with his arm, looking away from the statue which dominated the place. His eyes shed moisture, passionlessly; he hurt and he was tired and empty until he looked back at the statue which still beckoned.

Sbi had come; Sbi sat down by him. He thought of thirst and hunger when Sbi was there, needs which had begun to be obsessive with him, because he was unbearably empty, and the tremors had come back.

I shall die, he thought with a certain fatigued remoteness;

and remoteness failed him. He wept, wiped his eyes with a bandaged hand, simply sat there, and Sbi edged close and patted his knee. He flinched. "I can't take from you anymore," he said. "Sbi, it . . . upsets me. I can't do it. And I'm not sure I can walk anymore. Are we done? Is this the place? If you leave me here . . . I'm going to die."

Sbi said nothing. In time Sbi got up and walked away and Herrin watched him go, saying nothing, only despairing. There was only the statue then, aged, anomalous in the sea of hills and grass, giving no indication it had ever borne relationship to anything understandable. It offered love. It was only stone. He had sent Sbi away and Sbi had simply gone. The sun sank and the wind grew cold, and he listened to it in the grass and watched the change of light on the stone.

And then, at dark, a stronger whispering, and Sbi was back.

Herrin sat still, the wind cold on the tears on his face, and still did not hope, because whatever Sbi intended, Sbi's care of him was not sufficient to keep him alive, a simple mistake, a lack of comprehension.

Sbi came, squatted down, knees shoulder high as usual, held forth a small dead animal. "I have killed," said Sbi in a voice quivering and faint. "Herrin Law, I have killed a thing. Can you eat this?"

He considered the small furry animal, and looked from that to the distress in Sbi's eyes, sensing that the ahnit had done something on his behalf it would not, otherwise, have done. It looked, if ahnit could shed tears, as if it would. "Sbi, if we can get a fire, I'll try."

"I can make one," Sbi said, and set the little body down, stroked it as if in apology.

"It's not," Herrin asked in apprehension, "something of value to you."

"It was alive," said Sbi, ripping up grasses and digging a bare spot. "I don't wish to talk about it."

Sbi worked, furiously, hands shaking in an agitation Herrin had never seen in the ahnit . . . went off again for a prolonged time and came back again with sticks. Herrin watched in bewilderment as Sbi coaxed warmth, smoke, and then fire out of twirling wood, and then, comprehendng, bestirred himself to push grass over for Sbi to add. Fire crackled in the night, a tiny tongue of brightness in the cleared circle.

"In this place," Sbi mourned, and rose. "Eat. Please, when you are done, bury it. I don't want to watch."

Sbi fled. Herrin touched the small creature it had left, edged the limp, furry body close to the flames and suffered qualms himself, not knowing what to do with it but to push it into the fire and char it into edibility.

Oh, Sbi, he thought, trying not to inhale the stench or to think about what he was doing. Sbi had probably found a place remote from the smell and the memory. He swallowed the tautness in his throat and looked past the smoke to the statue under the moon, that mimed love. *Sbi.*

XXV

Waden Jenks: The University becomes your problem. We take the Outsiders in, and you instruct them. You'll have your ambition, Keye. The University; and through it the Outsiders who come here.

Master Lynn: The shaping of ten thousand years and more . . . of all time. Quite enough for me. Unlike Herrin, I don't meddle with the present. I don't make his mistake.

Waden Jenks: I regret him.

Master Lynn: Need him? I think not.

Waden Jenks: No. I regret him. That's different.

Master Lynn: (Silence.)

Herrin buried the remains, such as his crippled hands could not handle, and the skin and bones. He had a small store of meat, which he had stripped with his teeth—his fingers could not do it—and which he dried over the coals and hoped to keep. He felt sick in one sense, but better with something in his belly. The tremors had stopped. He dug with his booted heel and dumped the pitiful scraps into the pit, then smoothed the earth with the edge of his hand, soiling the bandage, which already was soiled, with grease. "Sbi," he called, and after a time, "Sbi!"

Sbi returned, pausing before the statue in an attitude of—offering, Herrin thought, watching the gesture. Tribute, perhaps, to a forgotten artist; or to a god who believed ahnit into reality.

Eventually Sbi came to him and sank down again.

"I'm all right," Herrin said. "Maybe I can walk now."

Sbi moved close to him and put a rangy arm about him. "No. Rest."

"For what, Sbi? Where do we go? To your own kind? Or is this where we stay?"

Sbi said nothing for a moment. "No. You tell me where you want to go."

"Sbi, why are you doing this?"

"Tell me where you want to go."

"Back to the city? Is that what you want me to say?"

"Tell me where you *want* to go."

He rested against Sbi and thought a while. "The river, higher up the river. There's a town called Camus. There's a valley up in the hills; a farm. I'd like to go there, Sbi."

"I know Camus," Sbi said.

"There," said Herrin.

"You came from this place."

"You know a great deal about me."

"Remember how long I've observed."

"I came from that valley. Yes. I want to go back there."

"All right," Sbi said.

No argument, no discussion. "You want something," Herrin surmised. "Is this it?"

"Go where you wish. I'll help you."

"Why?"

Sbi said nothing. But he had not expected answers from Sbi.

XXVI

---

*Waden Jenks: I informed you on Camden McWilliams;
if you're not having success, don't look to others.*

*Col. Olsen: The information was accurate beyond
doubt?*

*Waden Jenks: Colonel, what you doubt is at your
discretion.*

Col. Olsen: Reasoning with you people is impossible.

*Waden Jenks: You asked for information; I gave you
precise past patterns. You see the whole situation.
You complain to me about your lack of success.
Hardly reasonable.*

The pain grew less. There was a morning, a dewy, otherwise unpleasant morning when clothing was sodden, when the
bandages were somewhat looser, and Sbi so carefully began
to adjust the splinting, substituting slim green wands.

"They bend," Herrin said, and clamped his lips against the
pain as he tried to flex his right hand. "Sbi, they move."

"Yes," said Sbi, although the movement was more a tremor
than voluntary. Sbi avowed to have seen it, and kept to his
wrapping. "Try, whenever you think of it, try to bend the
hands."

"Not much hope, is there?" Herrin asked. "There'll not be
anything close to full use of them."

"Bend them when you can."

He nodded, sat patiently while Sbi worked on his hands.
Winced sometimes, because the pain was very much still
there when some jar set it off again. Sbi chewed a bit of grass
. . . incongruous to watch it disappear upward from stem to
bearded head and vanish; Sbi did not much eat the stems, but
chewed on them from time to time. Herrin had a bit of meat
tucked away, but would not eat it in front of Sbi, and a

139

handful of fire-parched grain which at least gave him no stomachache as the raw grain did.

"Here," said Sbi, leaning forward, touched him mouth to mouth and transferred a quick burst of sugary fluid, moisture without which he could not survive. Sbi had developed a deftness about the process which he greatly appreciated, so matter-of-factly performed it failed to bother him as it might.

"It doesn't hurt much," Herrin said, trying the newly bandaged hands. "That's good, Sbi. That's good."

"I hoped so," Sbi said. Sbi plucked another heavy-headed bit of grass and stuck it in his mouth. "Come, are you ready?"

With that they broke their camp, no more than picking themselves up off the ground. They did not use fire often. Sbi had no particular use for it . . . *it crumbles,* Sbi objected of parched grain; and: *There's always something,* to the question what ahnit ate when there was no grain ripe. Not animals, Herrin reckoned, never that; he tried this and that as they walked . . . and more than once Sbi stopped him before he picked some plant. "Deadly," Sbi would say, or: "You won't like that; very bitter."

"Don't you ever eat in the city?" Herrin wondered once.

"I fancy beer," said Sbi, "and cake."

Herrin thought of both and suffered. Of a sudden he thought of porridge, and cold mornings and warm beds; of sights and scents and sounds which came back together and had to do with home.

And that afternoon they came to the Camus valley, overlooking the town he remembered.

"It's there," he exclaimed; "it's *there,* Sbi."

And he started down the hill, tired as he was, remembering where a road was which led to home.

XXVII

John Ree: They say he's in the city. One of the invisibles.

Andrew Phelps: (looking about) We shouldn't talk about this.

John Ree: I'll tell you: we've hunted. Apprentice Phelps, I've hunted.

Andrew Phelps: Among them?

John Ree: Wherever he might be. Wherever.

The house was there, as he recalled, bare boards one with the color of the earth, a corrugated plastic roof . . . they did not even get the building slabs they had down in Camus. The windows were lighted in the evening. There was no better time to come home.

Herrin stopped on the hillside, in the midst of a step, and looked back at Sbi, who had stopped on the hillcrest. Ungainly, alien, robes flapping in the slight breeze, Sbi just stood, whether sad or otherwise Herrin could not tell. And then he thought of the midnight cloth he himself wore, the cloak, the bandages, which he had taken on him like a brand, which no one put off once on.

He shed the cloak and took it back, held it in his hands toward Sbi, there in the wind, on the hill. "Good-bye," he said, which curiously had more of pain in it than leaving that brown board farmhouse had had for him long ago, because there was so much of Sbi he had missed and never seen and there was so much Sbi had done that made no sense and now never might. He thought Sbi looked sad, but with Sbi's face that was no certainty. "Good-bye," he said a second time, and left the cloak in Sbi's hands and walked back down the hill.

Faster and faster.

He was tattered and worn, his Student's Black dusty and seam-split at the arm; his face was unshaven and his hair hung in dusty threads; the bandages remained on his hands—he could not have borne the pain without them—but the color was obscured by grease and dirt. Home . . . and cleanliness, and food, and most of all, to be what he had been. He almost ran as he approached the lighted windows and the door. "*Hello!*" he called, to make them listen, "Hello!" He reached the wooden door and hit it with his elbow, and listened in agonized excitement as chairs moved inside, as familiar furniture scraped on a familiar wooden floor and steps crossed to the door.

"Who's there?" It was his father's voice.

"It's Herrin," he cried. "Father, it's Herrin, home."

The door opened, a rattling of the latch, swung inward. His father was in the doorway, his mother beyond, both grayed and older than he remembered; he crossed the threshold, opened his arms although they had never had the habit of touching him, and if they embraced him it would hurt him—he would bear the pain of his ribs to ease that ache inside.

"What happened?" his father asked, looking frightened. "Where did you come from?"

"I'd like a drink. Something to eat."

They looked at him in evident disturbance. He stood still, letting them sort it out slowly, trying to remember as he had always remembered, that they thought differently and less deeply than he. After a moment his mother drew back a chair at the table in front of the door and joined his father who was busy in the small kitchen at the left of the table, virtually one room with the bedroom on the right.

It was small; it was poor; there was so little here that had changed over the years, except there was a new rug on the floor, and it was far newer and brighter than anything else in the room. Dishes rattled comfortingly. Even the feel of the chair was right, the table under his elbows what he remembered it felt like. There was the place on the other side of the door where his bed had stood. A plow leaned there now, probably waiting sharpening. Perrin's bed was still there, beyond theirs. It *smelled* right, the whole house, as it had always smelled; there was something about the spices they cooked with, that no one in the Residency kitchens and no one in University had the knack of. Food had always tasted better here.

His parents brought him a sandwich and a cup of tea, steaming hot, set it down in front of him. He took half the sandwich up in dust-crusted, bandaged hands and bit into it with a bliss that ran through his body, choked that bite down and handled the tea the same, a delicate sip of purest steaming liquid out of old, familiar dishes; for a moment he felt Sbi's lips and shuddered, and felt the old china again.

He ate, tears welling up from his eyes, because it was chill outside and warm inside, and the inside of him was coming to match it, filled with food and comfort. He could not eat all of it, could not possibly. And that seemed bliss beyond compare, to know that he need not be hungry, or thirsty.

Only then, his belly full to hurting, he began to notice the silence and their eyes, which waited for him, as they had waited in years long before, knowing that reasoning with him was not easy or often possible, on their level. The world had changed; they had not. He looked back at them, frightened by that old silence.

"What happened?" his father asked a second time. They were still waiting for that precise question. "Where did you come from?"

"Kierkegaard. I walked."

Silence. They stared at his face, not his hands, fixedly at his face, without expression on their own beyond a residual fear.

"I've come home," he said.

They said nothing to that.

"Why did you walk?" his mother asked.

"I've quit the University. Mother, there are Outsiders there. The First Citizen is bringing them in. I can't stay there. I don't want to stay there the way things are getting to be."

Fear. He still picked that up in the expressions. And something else, a deeper reserve.

"I need a bath," he said.

Without a word his mother nodded toward the back of the house where the bathroom was, where an old pump produced water with slow patience.

"I'm going to stay," he said.

"Heard you're a great artist, a University Master," his father said.

"Was," he said. "I quit."

There were nods, nothing of warmth, nothing of comfort in his presence.

"I've stopped all that. I don't belong to the University. I have nothing to do with it any longer. I want to stay here, to farm."

Nothing. Their faces were like a wall, shutting him out.

"Perrin's moved out," he asked, "has she?"

Silence.

"Is she here, then?"

"Perrin's dead," his mother said. It hit him in the stomach. Fantasies collapsed, a structure of new beginnings he had imagined with Perrin, an intent to do otherwise than he had done, a half-formed longing to enjoy a closeness he had thrown away without ever knowing it.

"What happened?" he asked.

"She couldn't be you. She killed herself the year you left. Everyone talked about you. Everyone was proud of you. Even when you were gone she had no place for herself. Except here. And that wasn't good enough."

He sat motionless.

"She left a note," his father said. "She said she had never had anything important. It was all for you, for University."

His eyes stung. He stared across the room at the wall while his parents quietly, together, rose from the table and took the dishes back to the kitchen. The tears slipped and slid down his face. He was not sure why, because he did not particularly feel them, more than that stinging and a leaden spot in his stomach which might as likely be the sandwich on an abused digestion, far more food than he should have eaten all at once.

"You're important," his mother said, drying her hands by the counter. "We heard all the way in Camus about that big statue, about how you're the most important man in the University. You can't want to live in Camus."

"I'm not that, anymore." He held up his bandaged hands. "*I had an accident.* It's all right to say something about it. I can't work anymore, not like that. I've come home to do a different kind of work."

There was dead silence. His parents stood there and stared bleakly at him. After a moment his father shrugged and walked over to the fireside where evening coals were left. "You'll make something important here in Camus . . . better you should go down to the town and work there. There's nothing up here for you."

"You're not listening to me."

"Mind like yours . . . I suppose you've come out here to start a whole new branch of the University. A whole new way. But that's nothing to us."

"Perrin was ours," his mother said. "Perrin was ours. We understood Perrin and she understood us. She wanted so much she didn't have. It wasn't fair. Perrin was *ours*. Nothing was fair with her. She hated Camus after you'd gone. Talked about Kierkegaard. Wanted to come to University. Couldn't. She wasn't talented like you. That was the way of everything, wasn't it? You're going to start to work in Camus now. What are you going to build there?"

"They're wrong," he said. He stammered on the words. "Everything, everything is *wrong*. They broke my hands, you hear me? I've *walked* to this house from Kierkegaard. They've brought in Outsiders from off the planet and they're doing things that are going to change everything and no one sees it. Do you know, these Outsiders pilfer, too? Right off the tables in the market, they walk away and people pretend they don't see because that's what they're supposed to do, and they play the game, but it's a hole to nowhere . . . those goods don't turn up in market again, they don't come back to Kierkegaard, not even to this *world*. It goes out from here. We've opened the door on something that isn't small enough for us. We *think* we know what's real and we don't. It's all a structure that's operable only if we all believe it."

They moved, his mother drying her hands which were already dry, and his father walking back to the kitchen counter as if he had business there.

"They're wrong," Herrin said again. "I've been through the system and I've taught in the system and I know the structure of the whole thing and it's wrong."

"Long wet autumn," his father said to his mother. "I think we've got to expect a cold winter."

"Father," Herrin said. "Mother?"

"Leaves have gone dark," his mother said. She looked through to the wall, still wiping her hands on the towel. "I think it's time to pull some of those tubers, take a look at them."

"Might."

"Can't afford a ground freeze. Could come any morning." She seemed to shrink, a slight shiver.

"Mother?"

There was no answer. They started putting away the dishes. Herrin sat, hands on the table, with the sandwich lying undigestible in his belly. He sat and watched in silence as they began stirring about the evening routine, the complaints about the quality of the wood for keeping the fire at night; the reminder about the kitchen fire and the old argument about the temperature in the room, something played for him, and in his absence. He watched, hungry for the sights and the sounds, nonparticipant. He rose finally when they were about to go to bed and searched out a towel and filled it with food, got a bottle for water and filled it from the kitchen tub; while they settled into bed he entered the bath, pawed through things until he found a razor, and soap, and he searched the closet for clean clothes, but his father was smaller than he and there was nothing of his own left. Just Perrin's things, still hanging there. He closed the door and snatched up the things he had pilfered, hastened past his parents' bed in the main room and out through the door.

He left it open, ran, stumbling and blind with tears. "Sbi," he called out, but he had said good-bye to the ahnit, had turned Sbi away. "Sbi," he wept, and ran up the hill clutching the bundles in his arms.

A shadow met him just the other side, Sbi's tall shape, Sbi's scent, Sbi's enfolding arms, which took him in, gently comforting. He wept, long; Sbi sat down with him on the grassy hillside and simply held him.

"They stopped seeing me," he said.

"Yes," said Sbi." I feared so."

He drew another breath, wiped nose and eyes with the back of his bandaged hand, blinked in the grit it left. "I pilfered things I could use."

"Good," said Sbi.

"I want to leave this place," he said.

"Yes," said Sbi, and rose, keeping an arm about him to help him. Something warm settled about his shoulders, the cloak Sbi had kept waiting for him. "'Where shall we go now?"

He shook his head. "I don't know. I don't know."

Sbi picked up the bundles of toweling, and laid an arm again about his shoulders. "Come. Out of the wind at least."

He came, settled where Sbi wished, a place still not out of Law's Valley, nor far enough from the house for his liking; but rocks sheltered it from the wind and he could sit down next Sbi and curl up with knees and elbows inside the midnight cloak.

There was dew the next morning too, but at least they were not hungry as well as cold and wet. Herrin breakfasted on parched grain and a bit of cheese . . . he offered a bit of bread to Sbi, but Sbi would not take it, for whatever reason. And he drank from the jar, the merest sip, which Sbi watched silently.

They packed up then. The house would have been visible, he thought, if he climbed the hill; he could have looked down on his father and mother's house by daylight . . . had he just walked up the rise. He would not. Sbi wove grass braids with great dexterity and bound up the bundles he had to carry. "Here," said Sbi. "We might go to Camus and pilfer a basket, but until we do. . . ."

"Not Camus," Herrin said. He leaned against the rock and hitched the grass rope to his shoulder, a weight on his hand for the instant, which hurt despite the splints.

"Where?" Sbi asked again.

He shook his head. "I don't care." He looked up, looked at Sbi's face, recalling that last night he had deserted Sbi. Sbi had waited. Dismissed, had simply sat down outside the house and waited last night. His own predictability disturbed him. All that he did assumed the nature of a pattern of Sbi's choosing. Sbi's reality.

"What do you want?" he asked of Sbi again. "You stay with me . . . why?"

No answer. He looked at the morning-lit face, the black, wet eyes, and found the morning bitter cold.

"Do what you like this time," he told Sbi. "Go to your own kind; I'll come with you, if that's what you ultimately want."

Sbi's lips pursed in one of those unreadable expressions. "That would be a far walk, Master Law."

"Where are your kind? Where do you live? What do you do with your lives?"

Silence.

"Sbi, what do you want from me?"

Again silence, which was like what his mother and father had done to him, and he did not find it comfortable. But Sbi put out an arm and embraced him very gently, beginning to walk from where they had camped. "I'll tell you," said Sbi, "that there are very few of us now. You brought us disease. Disease went where humans never have, into the far hills. We died in great numbers; but you never saw. It was a significant fact to us; but it wasn't real to you. We used to live in the hills, but we yielded up this valley. We were in awe of you . . . once. But I am educated in your University; and you never saw me. *That's* why we came, to learn the things you know."

He walked, not looking at Sbi, finding Sbi's embracing arm a heavier and heavier weight as they descended the hill. "What will you do with those things you know?"

Silence.

"Sbi, is that it? That you stay with me . . . because you think I can teach you something? Is that what you want from me?"

"No," Sbi said.

"What then?"

Silence. They walked the level ground now, making their way across the fields in the direction Sbi chose, back the way they had come into the pocket valley. Herrin thought, tried to reason, kept turning back to the thought of ahnit *in* the University, invisible in the halls. In the Residency. In the dome in the Square, where others had started seeing them.

Sbi embraced him still, keeping him warm, keeping him close. So Waden had done to him, lulling his suspicions, using his weakness to bypass his reason. That Sbi was doing so seemed only reasonable. There would be a time that Sbi had extracted all the use possible from him, but for the moment it was a convenient source of help. The difficult thing, he decided, was knowing when to pull away, when to elude such users before they had their chance to harm him.

But he did not know where to go.

The size of what Sbi wanted, he reckoned, had to be measured in terms of the discomfort Sbi was willing to tolerate to get it; and what Sbi wanted had to do with his own will, his own consent, or something beyond the physical, because anything other than that, Sbi could do.

He tried to reason around an alien mind, and there was no reason; he tried to reason what he himself wanted, which was formless. Mostly he was not afraid of the world when he was with Sbi; he was only afraid of Sbi, and that limited things to a visible, bearable quantity.

That day, Sbi led him out of the valley and again into the hills. Sbi stopped whenever he grew tired, and comforted him and kept him warm, which was the limit of what he asked. It was limbo, and Sbi seemed patient with it.

He slept that night in Sbi's arms, his belly comforted with pilfered food, his misery somewhat less than it had been; he thought again and again, half-sleeping, what pains Sbi had taken with him, and what inconvenience Sbi suffered, and he wondered.

Sbi hated him, possibly, for what he had made the ahnit do, in taking that small life.

But then the ahnit was not capable of killing him, and he did not easily imagine that Sbi meant to do something *to* him.

To do something *with* him, undoubtedly. Whatever use he had left in him that appealed to an alien mind. He thought of his own work in the heart of Kierkegaard, and of the lonely pair of figures in the hills which Sbi had so wanted him to see, and neither made sense.

Sbi's hand massaged his back, over tense muscles. "Pain, Master Law?"

"No." The voice had startled him. He had not known the ahnit was awake. It disturbed him and he tried to relax, while Sbi's hand massaged a spot which was particularly tense.

"You haven't slept much."

"Nor have you."

"I don't sleep as much as you."

"Oh," he said, and shut his eyes again and accepted the comfort, tired and puzzled at once.

"Master Law," said Sbi, "why did they cripple you?"

He stiffened all over. It was the Statement again; it was never, to Sbi's satisfaction, answered.

"I don't know, Sbi. What is it that I don't see?"

Silence.

"And how could you know?" he asked. "You weren't there.

You don't *know* Waden Jenks. How am I missing the answer?"

Silence.

"Waden—couldn't bear a rival. He warned me so."

"Why?"

"Why what?"

"Either. Why warn you?"

He thought about it. "It wasn't rational, was it?"

Silence.

It lay at the center of what he did not want to think about. He lay still, staring into the dark. "Sbi. Where do you want me to go? What do you want?"

Silence.

"Whatever you want," he said, "I'll do it. I don't see anything else. I don't see anywhere else. You don't make sense to me. I don't know why you're out here or why you bother or what you want. What is it?"

Silence.

"Sbi."

More silence. He grew distraught. Sbi patted him gently, as if trying to soothe him to sleep.

"Let me alone." He scrambled up, pushing with his hands, which hurt him, and stalked off close to striking at something, his bound ribs not giving him air enough. He stopped, staring out across the plains and finding nothing on the horizon but grass and night-bound sky, and stars, which belonged to strangers, the vast Outside, which went on and on, challenging illusions.

Suddenly he was afraid. He looked back, half expecting to find Sbi gone, or near him. Sbi simply waited.

And that did not wholly comfort him either.

XXVIII

Master Lynn: Where were you?
Waden Jenks: Where I chose. Is that your concern?
Master Lynn: You were out there again. In the Square.
  Consider your appearance. You pay homage to that
  thing. Your curiosity has you, not you it.
Waden Jenks: I find its counsel superior.
Master Lynn: He was your enemy. Do you consider
  that?
Waden Jenks: Are you my friend?
Master Lynn: Is anyone, Waden Jenks?

There was no particular direction. Sbi walked east, this day, and sat down after a time, munching a grass stem, and seemed content to sit. Herrin lay down full length on his back and stared at the clouds drifting, fleecy white and far, with such a weight on his mind that it seemed apt to break.

"Sbi," he said at last, "teach me."

"Teach you what, Master Law?"

"My name is Herrin."

"Herrin. Teach you what?"

"What reality is."

"What do you see?"

"Sky."

"What do you feel?"

"Pain, Sbi."

"Both are real."

"Whose reality?"

"Everyone's."

"What," he snorted, having finally discovered Sbi's depth, *"everyone's* forever and however far? That's hardly reasonable."

"Throughout all the universe."

151

"You're mad."

Silence.

"How can external events be real to you, Sbi?"

"I feel them."

It angered him. In frustration he slammed his hand against the ground and rolled a defiant look at Sbi, with tears of pain blurring his eyes. "You tell me you felt that."

"Yes. All the universe did."

Sbi proposed an insanity. He retreated from it, simply stared at the clouds.

"I've taught you," said Sbi, "all I know."

"You mean that I'm not able to perceive it."

"Where shall we go, Herrin?"

He bit down on his lip, thought, trying to draw connections through the maze of Sbi's logic. He gave up. "How long are you prepared to sit here, Sbi?"

"Is this where you wish to be, then?"

"What does it matter what I want?"

Silence.

"Sbi, I was wrong. I've spent my life being wrong. What can I do about it?"

Silence. For the first time he understood that answer. He turned on his side and looked at Sbi, who sat chewing on another grass stem. His heart was beating harder. "What were you waiting for all those years in the city? For me? For someone who could see you?"

"Yes."

"And what difference does it make whether I see you?"

Silence.

"It makes a great deal of difference, doesn't it, Sbi?"

"What do you think?"

"'That it makes everything wrong. That the whole world is crazy and I'm sane. Where does that leave me, Sbi?"

"Invisible. Like me."

He found breathing difficult, not alone from the bandage. He pushed himself up on his elbow. "You had to let me go back to my own house to find that out."

"I had no idea what would happen. Reality is not in my control. Nor are you."

"You'll wander all over Sartre taking care of me if that's what I decide, is that so?"

"I will stay with you, yes. And keep you from harm if I can."

"Why?"

Sbi sucked in the grain-bearing head and chewed it. "Because I want to. Because when you struck your hand I had the pain, Herrin."

"I could ask you; I could ask you question after question and when I got close to what I really want to know you'd say nothing."

"The important questions are for you to answer. It is, after all, your world that's in jeopardy; mine is long past that."

"Why were you among us?"

"If someone had destroyed your world, would you not have an interest in those who had done so?"

"They *did*. And I don't want to go back. I don't want to see them again or be seen."

Sbi simply stared at him.

There was no relief for the silence, none. He sat up with his bandaged hands in his lap and contemplated them, flexed his hands slightly against the splints and bit his lip at the pain which won him no great degree of movement.

"Who broke your hands, Herrin Law?"

He shut his eyes, weary of the repeated question.

"Why?" Sbi asked inevitably.

He shook his head slowly, drew a breath which suddenly stopped in his throat. His eyes unfocused. He thought to Fellows' Hall, a certain evening, and a conceit which had gripped them both, him and Waden. "I'd begun to see *you*. I'd begun to see things the way they were; and Waden was never dull. I think he saw too, Sbi. I think he did. He *does*. Sbi, I'm going back."

"Yes," said Sbi.

He had reached for the bundles of toweling and grass rope which were all his possessions; and suddenly he caught Sbi's expression, and Sbi's tone, and it was not the same as when he had proposed going to the valley. Then there had been disappointment, vague reluctance. Now it was different.

"You've pushed me to this," he said, wrapping his arms about the bundles and staring at Sbi. "Sbi, have I guessed enough of what you want? Or do you go on the way you have?"

"I don't know that you're right," Sbi said. "But your logic

seems irrefutable save by Waden Jenks. I will tell you what I want, Herrin. I have found it: a human who can see. I'll tell you what I've waited for all these years as you say . . . to learn what that human will do, when he sees. But one thing frightens me: what those who don't see will do to him."

"They won't be *able* to see me," he said, disliking Sbi's proposition. But he thought about it. "There are the Outsiders, aren't there? And they see."

"To my observation—yes."

He sank down off his heels and frowned with the pain and with the fear the pain set in him. He stared straight before him and thought about it for a long while.

"Now it's hiding," he said finally.

"How, hiding?"

"Before, I was surviving. Now it's hiding, staying up here in the hills. Now I don't go back because I'm afraid. Or if I don't go back I *am* afraid." He rolled a glance at Sbi. "You're good; you've had the better of me. You set it all up. Located the best of us . . . studied how to intervene. You had your best chance when I came out of the University and worked in the open. Then you could get to me. Accosted me in the dark that night, on Port Street. That *was* you. Drove Leona Pace over the edge. Came back to plague me. Worked at me—constantly."

"Yes," said Sbi.

"Now I should go back to the city. Now I should take on Waden Jenks and finish drawing him into this."

"Yes."

"*Why*, Sbi?"

"Our survival."

"Reasonable," he said, trying at least to admire the artistry of it.

"What are you going to do?"

He shook his head. "Surrender Freedom to your manipulation? That's what you've set me up to do, isn't it? Me, and Waden Jenks; one of us set against the other . . . myself, taken out of influence; and on the other hand given the chance to change the world. I'm one of the invisibles. It occurs to me that murder is possible for one of us. That I can push Waden over the edge . . . I can do that, because I've nothing to lose, have I? Or I can sit here in the hills and know that the greatest thing I ever did fitted your purpose."

"All that humans have done is bent around us, Herrin Law. The way you live, the pains you take to ignore us, the insanity which claims some of you . . . are these things spontaneous? Were you ever—reasonable?"

He stared at the horizon, colder and colder. "No," he said.

"Herrin. I'll go *with* you. I'm concerned for you."

He thought of the statue in the hills; of a small dead creature in Sbi's hands; of Sbi's hands caressing what Sbi had killed.

Of his parents going about their business not seeing him.

He rested his face against the back of his hand, wiped at the left eye. "So, well, tell me this, Sbi, what do you expect to happen?"

"I don't know. But it will be of human choosing, and my choosing, both, my friend. Both at once. Is it not reasonable?"

It was, as Sbi said, reasonable. "I've taught students," Herrin said. "I thought I knew, and thought I saw, and I taught. For them, I'm going back, and Waden . . . I don't know about Waden." He struggled to his feet, started to bend for his belongings again, but Sbi anticipated him and caught them up.

"It's not far," Sbi said.

He had guessed that too, that Sbi had brought him generally in the direction Sbi wanted him to go.

XXIX

Waden Jenks: Do you know what frightens me most in the world, Herrin? Not dying. Discovering—that I'm solitary; that my mind is the greatest one, and that I'm damned to think things beyond expression, that I can never explain to any living being. Have you ever entertained such thoughts, Herrin?
Master Law: (Silence.)

Waden Jenks: I think you have, Herrin. And how do you answer them?

Colonel Olsen: The module's come through; the station begins its construction. Now there's a matter of the other agreements. Of supply. My aides will draw up a list of requirements.

Waden Jenks: Of no interest to me. Consult appropriate departments in the Residency.

Colonel Olsen: We find no cooperation in these departments of yours.

Waden Jenks: You intrude, colonel; we have our ways. You persist in coming in person. Use the liaisons we are training in University; that's their purpose, after all.

Colonel Olsen: Nothing you've given us has been of value; not your information; not your promises of co-operation.

Waden Jenks: Yet you remain; you and I both know you are obtaining something you desire: a base. Supplies have become important to you. Let's then admit that you want them badly and that it's a matter for my personal attention; let's adjust the price accordingly. Let's talk about agreements that keep your bureaus from disturbing us. From setting foot here.

Colonel Olsen: We have policies. . . .

Waden Jenks: They don't get you what you want.

A ship passed in the night sky, a shuttle, headed offworld. Herrin watched it go, from the hills above Kierkegaard. He looked down on the city, with its dimly lighted streets, with the bright glare of the port like a bleeding wound. He felt Sbi's presence at his elbow without needing to look. "Do you know what that was, Sbi?"

"One of the shuttles. I know. You taught us about other worlds."

"Does it occur to you that we two don't control everything?"

"Ah, Herrin, I understand more than that."

"What more, Master Sbi?"

"That somewhere among those points of light stand others

who misapprehend their limits; that somewhere at this moment someone is in pain; that somewhere a life has begun; that somewhere one has ended; I feel them all tonight."

"I'm trying to feel them."

"Somewhere," said Sbi, "is someone else wrestling with dilemma. Somewhere is someone wondering the value of life itself. The universe is always asking questions."

"Somewhere," said Herrin, "someone is scared."

"Beside you, Herrin Law."

He turned and looked at the ahnit, who almost blended with the night, a shadow among shadows. A strange impulse possessed him, a melancholy; he opened his arms and embraced Sbi's alien shape, gently, because contact hurt. He had done so in his life with his parents, with his sister when they were both small; with Keye when he made love; with Waden when Waden had a public gesture to make; with the workers when they helped him from the scaffolding . . . only those times in his life had someone touched him; and with Sbi again it was different. Sbi embraced him very gently, and he stepped back and looked at Sbi sadly. "I don't see you have any need to go down there."

"Probably you don't see," Sbi said. "In some things you're very complicated. Why did you go to your old house, Herrin Law, and to those people?"

"I don't know."

"A Master does something and confesses not to know why?"

"I wanted shelter. It didn't quite work out, did it?" Heat came to his face. "I've made that mistake several times; it brought me here. Possibly it's got hold of me again. Why else am I going down there? Stubbornness. I have some perverse desire to try it again, to talk to people I knew, to shake them till they see. I'm sure the Outsiders will see. I'm sure those who did this to me will." He thought a moment. "I'm mad, aren't I? Invisibles are. So why should you go?"

"Why did you go to your old house, and to those people?"

"Not satisfied with my answer?"

"No."

He folded his arms across his ribs and stared at all the lights. "Well, it doesn't make sense."

And after a moment: "Why go, Sbi? Answer *my* questions."

"But this is what I've lived my life for."

"What, 'this'? What *this?*"

Sbi rested a hand on his shoulder. "That you give me back my faith. That I see our destroyers have the capacity to create. For one who believes in the whole universe, to one who doesn't . . . how can I explain?"

Herrin looked up at the sky above the city.

"We've become part of it again," Sbi said.

"And if we all die, Sbi? Somewhere in your universe, somewhere out there—is there some world dying tonight?"

"Do you feel so?"

"O Sbi." He shivered, and shook his head. And started down the slope, losing sight of the city among the hills.

Sbi overtook him, a soft pacing beside him in the grass, company in the dark.

"I don't think," Sbi said, "that the port market is likely to be open. The Outsiders were unfriendly to it. And without it—invisibles will go hungry; and some will pilfer in-town and some will trade for what those pilfer; and some who are ahnit will have gone away."

"Best they should," he said glumly. He considered what he should do, what there was to say . . . to Waden Jenks.

Try reason again? He had no doubt that Waden could kill him. Likely there were Outsiders about who would never let him close enough to say anything at all. They walked among the hills a long while, back and forth among the troughs and through the sweet-smelling grass. He savored the time finally, for what it was, because of the grass and the smell and the sounds and the hills and the sky. And Sbi's presence. That too.

Then he rounded the shoulder of a hill and had a limited view of the city again, faint jewels against the dark.

And some of them were red.

"Sbi?—Sbi, what do you make of that?"

"The port," Sbi said.

"It's not fire. It's not that." The lights flashed. There was a whole cluster of them. The unwonted sight disturbed him. It was an Outsider phenomenon. He recalled the shuttles which had lifted, more activity than Freedom had ever had from Outsiders. He thought of Waden, and increasingly he was afraid—for Waden, for Keye, for all of them down there who had started to disturb more than they knew how to see.

"Let *me* go to explore this thing," Sbi said. "I know where to go, how to move and when to move. Let me go ask questions. Some of us will have seen this thing close at hand."

"No," he said at once, and started off again, hurrying. "No, we're both going. I have a place to go, too, and questions to ask, and I know where to ask them."

"A ship," said Sbi. "Herrin Law, look, see it."

Something was lifting from the port. He began to laugh, a breath of relief. "A launch, that's all. Maybe it looks like that from up here."

"No," said Sbi. "I've seen, and it doesn't."

The ship climbed, shot off with blinking lights.

And exploded.

"*Sbi!*"

"I see," the ahnit said.

The flower died in the heavens. Suddenly there were bursts on land, flares which curled up silent, firelit smoke that traced toward the city.

Herrin began to run, downhill. "Wait," Sbi called to him, hastening after. Herrin ran, slid, slowed when his ribs shot pain through him and shortened his breath . . . he walked then, because that was all he could do, and the bursts of fire continued, stitching their way through Kierkegaard.

"Waden's Outsiders," he mourned to Sbi. "Waden's ambitions . . ."

XXX

Colonel Olsen: *(by com) That's Singularity. You'll be gratified to know, First Citizen, that we've finally found McWilliams and his lot. So much for your information.*

Waden Jenks: *(by com) Do something.*

Colonel Olsen: *Oh, we got him, First Citizen. That's a certainty. Only how many others are there?*

Waden Jenks: (Silence).
Colonel Olsen: First Citizen, what damage to landing fa-
 cilities?
Waden Jenks: (Silence.)

There were fires, in the grass, a wall of fire which swept
away to the sea, a curtain of red and orange two stories high
that made black skeletons of trees and bushes and glared eerily
in the water of the Camus.

There were fugitives, who straggled away from the city
along the Camus-Kierkegaard road, and crossed the bridge
over the firelit waters. Some were terribly burned, in shock;
some, perhaps mad, had flung themselves into the river and
drifted there, dark pinwheels in the red current.

"Stop,'" Sbi pleaded, catching gently at Herrin's cloak.
"Stop and consider."

Herrin did not, but wove his way across the concrete
bridge of the Camus, past scarecrow figures headed away,
past a cloaked figure who reached out hands and caught at
his companion, telling Sbi something in urgent booms and
hisses. Herrin delayed, wanting Sbi if Sbi wanted to stay with
him—saw Sbi accept the other's cloak and fling it on, bid the
other some manner of farewell, but the other ahnit, naked of
the cloak, stood staring as Sbi came away to go with him.
"It's bad in the city," Sbi said. "Some of the buildings are
afire."

He had reckoned so. He thought of his work, vulnerable in
the center of the city, and hastened along the paved highway.
It occurred to him that another burst of fire could come
down on them at any time. He looked up as they walked and
saw nothing but the smoke, the stars obscured.

Breath failed him finally, where the road bent from the
riverside, where the buildings began and he could see the city
streetlights dark as they had never been, and fire. He saw the
dome, distant from him, outlined against burning, and stood
there, trying to get his wind. There were no fugitives here. He
could see figures beyond, but those who were running for the
highway had already run. Here, from this perspective up
Main from the highway, there was only himself and Sbi, Sbi
a reliable, comforting presence.

"Herrin," Sbi said quietly. "Herrin, were they weapons and
not some accident?"

"I think they were." He drew a deep and painful breath. "Waden said . . . of a certain man . . . that he could level the city. It's not so bad as leveled, Sbi, but it's all gone wrong; and whatever I could do—it's too late. Waden's new allies haven't helped. And I don't think my people will want this reality."

"They'll *see*."

"They'll go mad. They'll not survive this."

"I thought," said Sbi, "that ahnit had learned all the bitter things humans had to teach. I had not imagined this."

"Come on. Come on, Sbi, or go back. This can't be what you waited so long to find. Maybe I'd better go from here on my own."

"No," said Sbi, and stayed with him.

He walked slowly in the dark streets, deserted streets, with pebblestone and concrete buildings, faces all alike, eyeless black windows, open doors likewise black. Ahead of them a wall of flame burned in the city, outlining the dome and everything beyond. "It's the hedge," Herrin realized suddenly. "The hedge is burning, up by the Residency, the University. . . ."

So was a building close to them, somewhere near First and Main, beyond the dome, a steady spiral of firelit smoke. A warehouse, perhaps, or something more tragic: apartments were everywhere.

The dome was before them. Fire showed through the perforations here and there like tears of light. There was, even here, a wound, a fall of broken stone where the outermost shell of the dome was damaged. Herrin saw it and ached, walking across the paving and up to the entry and within.

People huddled here, citizens, invisibles . . . there was no telling in the deep shadow; the dome had become a shelter. Children wept, setting off bell-like echoes, a cacophony of mourning and sad voices. Herrin walked through, and Sbi with him, past the outer, triple shell and the curtain-walls, into the central dome, where the face of Waden Jenks survived untouched. Fire provided the light through the perforations now, dim and baleful, and cast the features into torment.

Herrin shut his eyes from the sight, looked back at Sbi's hooded form, saw beyond him dark masses of refugees. His own workers would be among them. If anyone would have come here, they would have come, as they always had. Fearfully he lifted his clumsy hands, pushed back his hood, knowing well the enormity of what he was doing; but they had seen far worse tonight than an invisible's face.

"Gytha," he called out, setting off sharp echoes which shocked much of the other echo into silence. "Phelps?" And because he committed other unthinkable things: "Pace? Are *you* here?"

Master Law, some voice said, somewhere in the dome. There was a flood of echoes, other voices whispering it, and one calling it out . . . "Master Law!"

People came to him, some that he knew, some that he did not, and suddenly he panicked, because in the dark there was no color, and he had deceived them. They came, and near him Sbi stood, still hooded. Someone tried to take his hand, and he flinched and saved himself, looked into Carl Gytha's tear-streaked face and flung his arms about him, which hurt too. He could not make himself heard if he tried: the whole dome rang with voices. *Master Law!* the shout went up, and people surged in until they pressed on him and Gytha and someone thrust at the crowd trying to clear him room.

"Let me out," he pleaded of Gytha, of Sbi, of anyone who could hear him. He shouted into the noise and could hardly hear himself. "Let me out!" The whole place was mad and Waden Jenks's firelit face presided over it in rigid horror.

Perhaps Gytha understood. A tide started in the press which surged toward the other side of the dome, which swept him along with Gytha's arm to protect him . . . or Sbi's . . . in the confusion he was no longer sure. The crush compressed his ribs, threatened his hands, and he would have fallen but for an arm which encircled his waist and pulled him.

They broke forth into the air, a spill of the crowd like a wound bleeding forth onto the firelit paving. He had a momentary view of the distant, dying fires of the hedge, of ancient shrubbery gone skeletal and black as winter twigs.

"Sir," someone was saying to him, but he shook his head dazedly, finding even breathing hard. The crowd was pouring out after him, threatening to surround him here as well. Panic took him and he pushed at someone with his arm, saw Gytha's anxious look directed to the outpouring crowd.

And there in shadow, a taller, hooded figure, which unhooded itself and stood with naked head facing the crowd, which wavered, which slowed. Sbi turned and purposefully came and took him by the arm, drew him away in the moment's shock, even away from Gytha, even from those he would have wanted to see. He yielded to Sbi's encircling arm, walking farther up Main, slipping into what fitful shadows there were from the light of the burning, where Second Street offered them shelter.

Herrin stopped there, sank down on the doorstep of a dark and open doorway, his arm locked across his aching side.

"You are hurt?" Sbi asked him, touched his face with two gentle fingers, wiped sweat from him.

"Drink?" Herrin asked, for shock threatened him and somewhere—he could not even remember where—he had lost the bundles of his belongings, everything. Sbi bent and touched his lips, transferred a mouthful of sweetish fluid to him, caressed his brow in drawing away and regarded him with great black eyes, pursed mouth bearing an expression of ahnit sorrow.

"Sit," Sbi wished him. "O Herrin, sit still."

"Waden," he said. "He and Keye . . . won't know what to do. Can't know what to do. I have to go to the Residency, Sbi, and talk to them . . . if I can help there—I have to."

He tried to get up. Sbi did not help him at first, until he had almost made it and almost fallen, and then Sbi's arm encircled him. A dark runner passed them, slowed, looked back and ran on, quick steps fading. Soon there were others, straggling after. Sbi's arm tightened protectively. "I don't trust this, Herrin."

"Come on. Come on. Let's get back to Main, into the light."

"Your species frightens me."

"Come." He walked, insisting, anxious himself until they were back on the main line of the city, with the smoldering hedge in front of them and the fire from the burning buildings still lighting the smoke which hung over the city like a reddened ceiling, casting light to all that was below it. It all looked wrong; and then he realized that he had never seen the buildings on Port Street without the façades lit. Only a few windows showed light on the Residency's uppermost floor. He could not see the University clearly, but they had emergency power over there too, as they did at the port, and it was all dark, as far as he could see.

He was afraid . . . on all sides, afraid. More runners passed them, one screaming: he thought it screamed his name, and flinched. Back at the dome they were still shouting, still in uproar, and the echoes made it like the voice of some vast single beast.

They left the concrete for the berm, which was powdered black with the burning of the hedge. Smoke obscured their vision. Fires still crackled, knee-high flames in a line down the remnant of the hedge on either side as they passed what was left of the archway and crossed onto Port Street, in front of the Residency.

The whole west end was a shambles, the roof of the fifth level caved in, making rubble of that level and the next, where he had had his rooms . . . and cracking walls beneath. The east wing, the source of the lights, stayed apparently intact, but the cracks ran there too.

I would have died here, he thought dazedly, reckoning where his rooms were. He crossed the street with Sbi close beside him. No one prevented them, no one appeared on the street or on the outside steps. The doors gaped dark and open, showing only a little light from somewhere up the interior stairs when they walked in. The desk at the entry was deserted, dusted with fallen cement and there was rubble on the floor.

"Waden?" he called aloud, and his voice echoed terrifyingly in the empty halls. Something moved, scurried, ran, stopped running in some new hiding. The skin prickled on his nape, and he felt the touch of Sbi's hand at his arm as if Sbi too were insecure. He started up the stairs, careful in the shadows and the litter of rubble. Sbi imprudently put a hand on the wooden railing and it tottered and creaked.

They came into the uppermost hall, where light showed on the right and wind from the ruined west wing came skirling in with a stinging breath of smoke. "Waden?" Herrin called again, fearing to surprise whatever guards Waden Jenks might have about him. He trod the hall carefully, toward that closed door where Waden's office was.

He called again. Something moved inside. He heard a voice, used his bandaged hand to press the latch and pushed it open.

Keye met them. She had been sitting opposite the door in the long room, and rose, and her hands came up to shield her face. She cried out: *Keye* . . . cried aloud, and Herrin reached out a hand to prevent her dissolution. "Keye," he said, but she darted—for him, he thought for the instant—and then slid past him, past Sbi, for the dark hall, out, out of his presence and the sight of him. He looked back again to the room, dazed and of half a mind to go after Keye, to stop her if he could and reason with her if there was any reason. But there was movement in the doorway beyond the ell, and Waden was there, his face quickly taking on that look that Keye's had had.

"Waden," Herrin said, before he could do what Keye had done. "What happened?"

Waden only stared at him, in frozen stillness.

"The Outsiders," Herrin said. "Waden, you see me. You see I'm not alone; you always have, haven't you? Wake up and see what's going on, Waden. The city's afire; your Outsiders have run mad. It was a lie. From the beginning, everything University set up—was a lie."

"Your reality," Waden said from dry lips. "This is your reality, Herrin Law."

He blinked, caught up in that fancy automatically, for one mind-wrenching instant that made all the walls shimmer, that rearranged everything and sent it inside out. "No," he said, and reached his clumsy hand for Sbi, for a blue cloak, drawing the ahnit forward, into Waden's full view. "Real as I am, Waden; real as you are, as the fire is real. You can't cancel it."

"It's yours," Waden said bleakly. "*I* would not have imagined this. I failed to kill you, and you did this."

"You're mad," Herrin said. "*I* did this? I did nothing of it. It was your doing, from the first time you brought them here. What ship attacked us? Was it *Singularity*? Or your own allies?"

"Whatever you imagine," Waden said. It was a lost voice, a lost look in his eyes, which spilled tears. "I should have had them finish you; I *needed* you. That should have warned me where control was . . . really. O Herrin, your revenge is excessive. Remake it. Revise it."

It was an ugly thing to see, a hurtful thing. He closed his eyes to it and looked again, saw Waden still standing there, hands open, face vulnerable. "I wish I could, Waden. But you see—" He sought, half humorous, some logic to devastate logic, to break through to Waden Jenks. "—I let it go. The reality I imagined was a reality that would become universal, that would exist on its own in time and space . . . that I myself could no longer interrupt, *that's* what I imagined. And now the world has to take its course under those terms. Sbi exists. We'll all see each other. We'll listen to the ahnit and see them. We'll not do things the way they were; we'll not teach dialectic to shut down minds; we'll not *be* what we were. And I can't stop it. That's what I imagined."

Waden's eyes were terrible. Not vacant . . . but following that speculation, gazing into possibilities. "What do you imagine that *I'll* do?"

"I imagine . . . that you'll do things that are natural to this reality. Whatever they are. I can't stop it. You can't. We have no more control, Waden. Nor do the ahnit. We share this world and it comes down to that. It has its own momentum and it can't be canceled."

Waden turned away, fending himself from the door frame, walked back into the dark.

"Waden," Herrin objected.

"You created paradox." Waden's voice came back out of the dark. "And you abdicated. You've done this, Herrin Law, you've done this."

Herrin started forward, to go in, but Sbi's arm intervened. "No," Sbi said. "No, don't go in there. Come with me. Please, come away from this place. *Now*."

Herrin shivered, and stopped, lost in his own paradox.

"*Come*," Sbi insisted, and drew him away, out the hall beyond the ell, into the corridor outside. He remembered Keye then and looked to all the shadows, half expecting her to be there.

Sbi drew him farther, toward the stairs, and down them, where the wind skirled in with the taint of smoke.

He hurried, wakened by the shock of the wind, hastened to be quit of the place and Waden's fancies, his reasoning which threatened to swallow up all the things he thought he knew, down and down the rubble-littered stairs, deeper and deeper into the dark. His breath came short. Sbi gripped his arm to keep him steady and kept his pace.

Something started in the dark; a running shape pelted from the floor below to the staircase and down again.

"Keye!" he shouted, making echoes. "Wait for me! Listen to me!"

The steps retreated, defying his control, racing away into their own reality.

And wood splintered, and crashed down in hideous echoes. *"Keye!"*

He ran, almost fell himself at the turn where the railing had broken, where it hung now, swinging in the almost dark, and a black-clad body sprawled on the steps below.

Sbi made to protest his haste, but he caught his balance against the wall and made the last turn down, dropped to his knees to try to lift Keye from where she had fallen on her belly, touched her shoulders and realized his hands had no strength to lift . . . and that lifting might kill her. He patted her shoulder helplessly, leaned to see her side-turned face, at once overwhelmed to realize life in the eyes and a breath beneath his hand.

"Keye. It's Herrin, Keye."

"No, it isn't," the answer came. Her lips hardly moved and the sound was no more than a whisper. "I cancel all your realities. And my own. And my own. And all the world."

The lips stopped moving and the breath sighed out. In an instant more the body diminished, a looseness very different from sleep.

He drew his hand back, recoiled slowly. He had never seen death happen. It seemed to take something of himself away too.

But the universe stayed.

Because, he wondered, he had indeed abdicated it? Because there was paradox, and he had made it? He knelt there, fixed in the thought, and Sbi gathered him to his feet and drew him away.

"Herrin," Sbi said when they were outside, on the steps and in the wind. Sbi hugged him tightly, till the ribs hurt, and set him against the wall and touched his face. "Herrin. Don't lose me. Listen to me."

"I hear you," he said. It was hard to speak, to pull his reason back from that logic that tried to claim it. He focused on Sbi's dark eyes, on Sbi's expressions which he had *learned* to read, and which he had never understood; on a remote monument which had stood before man had come to Freedom.

He looked up, above the door.

Man, said the inscription, *is the measure of all things.*

"No," he said.

There was a lightening in the east, down the ruins of Port Street, and it showed the University intact at least from this perspective. And the city . . . always before, the hedge had separated the Residency and the Outsiders from the city. A view was open now which had never been there before.

It was not fire in the east, but the sun coming up. He gazed at it in fixation, thinking that the world had turned, and that the greater forces in the Universe existed, as the star came up visible over the curve of the world with no one able to affect it.

There was argument which might prevail against that reasoning; he refused to pursue it, only staring toward the daylight as toward a goal that had to be won. "It's there," he said to Sbi. It was a horrid dawn, smoke-fouled and revealing ugliness, but it was the light, and it was coming.

XXXI

Herrin Law: Why go, Sbi? Answer my questions.
Sbi: But this is what I've lived my life for.
Herrin Law: What, "this" What this?
Sbi: That you give me back my faith. That I see our
*   destroyers have the capacity to create. For one who*
*   believes in the whole universe—to one who doesn't*
*   . . . how can I explain? . . . We've become part of it*
*   again.*

The sun kept coming, making real the cindered hedge, the building which still poured a twisting column of black smoke, but a wind had come with the dawn, and began to sweep away what had hung there. They walked into the long expanse of Main together, cloaked but unhooded, both of them. There was debris left from the night, paper, scraps of clothing, wisps of cindery stuff like pieces of the night left over, which blew lightly along the pavement and collected in the gutters and against the lee side of buildings.

And there were some who lay dead. Herrin stopped by each, to know whether this man, this woman, this boy or girl was in fact dead, or lay in shock, or unconscious, or helpless with injury. *He* had lain helpless once and only Sbi had seen him. But he and Sbi this time found none to help.

They saw the living, too, furtive shapes which flitted from building to building, shadow to shadow in the dawn, some cloaked and some in the plain clothes of citizens who had once—before the night—been sanely blind.

There were ahnit, a few, who glided among the shadows, and one who came out from a vacant doorway and, seeing Sbi, spoke a few quiet hisses and clicks. Sbi answered. That one slowly unhooded and walked away down the steps and around the corner and on through the streets.

"Tlhai," Sbi said. "Tlhai says some of us have stayed. That some have taken the injured away. That some have gone away, but may be back. We have the habit of this city. I think they'll come."

Herrin looked about him, at two or three of the human fugitives who had stood to stare in the shadows, but when he looked they ran away, and others came, and did the same.

"Stop," he called to them. They did so, some of them, three or four, some distance down intersecting Second Street. They looked at him, and seemed likely to run away. But when he walked a few paces on down Main, showing no intent to force his presence on them, they drew a few paces closer.

Others came, and still others. They looked from the windows, and peered out from dark doorways. . . . They crept down steps into the daylight, their clothes stained with soot and dirt, their persons disheveled. Sbi drew closer to him, touched a hand to his back. He turned half about and saw more of them from another direction.

His heart beat in panic. He tried not to show it, but when another glance back the way they had come showed them now surrounded, he despaired of himself and of Sbi. He had felt violence, which was in Kierkegaard, like seeing invisibles; such things did not happen . . . visibly. But there was no retreat out of this reality.

"Come," he said to Sbi. Up against invisibles, one just . . . walked, quietly past. He headed the way they had been going, which must take him through some of them, and they showed no disposition to back away.

They did not stop him. They all turned to keep their eyes on him but they offered no harm. "Master Law," one said. "Master Law," others murmured, and at his back he felt others following.

More gathered. He looked aside, and back, and faced a throng of solemn faces, expectant faces, haggard with desires and fears and every sort of need.

"The city still exists," he said, meaning that Kierkegaard still had people, still had needs and life of its own, but he saw the faces which drank that in desperately and realized what he had said to them, saw hope struggling there. They wanted to hear him. Perhaps, he thought, to them he was all they could find of the authority that had defined what was. A University Master. That was what they had found. They waited for reason, and the only reason he knew on their terms was paradox, that had swallowed Waden Jenks.

He could, he thought, destroy them. They came for answers and he could tell them lies.

"I've no answers for you," he said and saw that hope painfully wounded. "But—" He reached for something, anything to give them, because the need was so unbearably intense in that place, all about him, stifling breath. "—I know other things. I've seen a place . . . not so far from here . . . where other things exist. Where I've seen what's old. There's a place in the hills where a statue stands, all alone, but it goes on existing in the middle of all that grass and the bare hills. It goes on saying what someone created it to say, all by itself. I've seen it. It has to do with love, and it's out there all alone with no one to see it. Listen to me," he said, but there was no need to say: the crowd grew, in utter silence, with eyes fixed painfully fast on him. He needed no loud voice. "We were just born. All of us. We were new, this morning. We've gotten through the night and the sun's up even though we doubted it. Ahnit are here, and we are, and maybe Outsiders will come back. I think there'll not be another attack; there was a man named McWilliams who had cause for what he did . . . I think it was he, but there are other Outsiders, and likely they've done for him. There's not been another attack,

so someone out there either went away or couldn't do it
again. Go out in the city. Find everyone who *can* see, and
tell them the sun's come up. And it's all right to see."

The silence hung there. He walked away through it, his
hand resting on Sbi's shoulder, and people moved aside for
them. Some flitted away; some followed still.

"Master Law," said a man. It was Andrew Phelps. Herrin's
heart wrenched, recalling the mob, but Phelps's look was
sane, and anxious. "They said you were hurt," Phelps said.

He reached out his bandaged hand, very carefully, and
Phelps only let it rest on his, not closing on it. "It hurt," he
said. "But it's not so much, Phelps. They thought it was, but I
don't. Can you find the others? Can you bring them? There's
more than statues to make here. There's so much to *do*,
Phelps."

Andrew Phelps stood there, his mouth trembling, and looking as he used to when he had gotten some new instruction
. . . a moment to take it in, and then an eagerness. "To *do*,
Master Law?"

Herrin nodded. "Sir," Phelps said, and gently gave back his
hand, and hesitated a moment before he hastened off.

"Master Law!" they began to shout from house to house,
and people came and did nothing more than touch him. He
flinched at first, and then understood himself as a reality they
wanted to test; some touched Sbi as well, and fled in dismay.
The touches became more and more, until it seemed everyone
who met them on the street wanted to lay hands on them,
and Herrin grew afraid, because even little jolts could cause
him pain, and one of them might try to take hold of him too
violently. Hysteria swirled about him.

"Sbi," he said. "Sbi, stay close to me."

"They chase their own fears," Sbi said. "Ah, Herrin, I'm
afraid for you."

They had come to the dome itself, where others poured
out, and more gathered from other streets. They pressed in,
each pushing the others, until one did seize him, embraced
him, sobbing; and another did, and they hurt him, for all that
Sbi tried to fend them off: they were as anxious to touch Sbi
as well. *"No!"* Herrin shouted, and somehow and by someone
he found himself shielded, was taken by yet another pair of
arms, but gently this time, protecting him, and a second pair,
while people he knew were suddenly between him and the

crowd, making a ring about him and giving him and Sbi a place to stand.

Gytha was there, and John Ree. And more and more of them. There was Andrew Phelps, shouldering his way through the quietened crowd. From another quarter a blue-robed figure pressed forward, hood flung back from brown hair and broad, freckled face. Herrin saw her, held out his hand fearing someone would stop her. "Leona Pace," others of the workers murmured, and hands went out to pat her shoulders as she passed. "Apprentice Pace," others whispered, because the name was one set in bronze, ahead of all the others. Herrin put his arm about her, looked into a plain face, radiant through tears. Others cheered her. There were others who unhooded. Here and there in the crowd someone recognized someone lost and found again. There were names cried out, and tears shed. Some hunted those they remembered. "Mari," a man called out forlornly. "Mari, are you there, too?" Whether an invisible named Mari heard, Herrin did not learn, the noise of the crowd was too great, the press too insistent.

"Be still," he called out, close to exhaustion, and others tried to pass the word, a confusion of shouting until finally the noise was subdued.

"Ask them to sit down," Sbi said. It was inspiration. He did so, and uncertainly the word passed and people settled where they were on the pavement, disheveled and exhausted, many holding onto one another. Herrin still stood, and Sbi, and Gytha and Phelps and Pace.

He talked to them, in a silence finally so profound he need not shout. He said much that he had said before. "Don't be afraid," he told them. "Not of the ahnit, not of Outsiders, not of anything. Clean up your homes, clean up the streets, share with anyone who needs food or help. If anyone lacks shelter . . . there are rooms in the University; there's shelter there. See everything. *Do* something when something needs doing. That's all."

He was very tired. He thought if he did not get away soon he would fall down where he stood, senseless. His vision kept going gray and the sunlight blurred. He put out a hand for Sbi's help, and Sbi put an arm about him. So did someone else, and the others cleared a way for him, parting the crowd, which stayed seated, all but the narrow aisle dislodged. There was a murmuring, and finally others gained their feet, a wave spreading from that disruption, but they did not rush in on him.

They found him a place to rest, on the steps of a building. People brought blankets, and food and drink, and he sat there with Sbi and Leona Pace and Gytha and some of the others, but most of the workers were out cleaning up the Square, out investigating shelter in the University, wherever he sent them. Some went to the port to order the market opened.

He slept a time, cradled in Sbi's safe arms, and, on the edge of sleep, knew that people walked soft-footed up to be sure that he was all right. Those with him hushed them and sent them away.

But finally there was a thunder in the heavens, and cries filled the streets. Herrin waked and looked up. "Something's landed," Carl Gytha said. "Master Law, we have to get you out of here."

"No," he said after thinking about it. "No. They can come if they like." He laid his head down again against Sbi, and shut his eyes.

And in time the visitors came, blue-clad, walking with rifles down the center of Main. People began to come there, anxiously, betraying him by trying to protect him. He was aware of it all, still resting but with eyes open.

"Come *on*," Leona Pace pleaded with him. "Please. They'll hold them."

"No. I have no anonymity anymore. They'll have been to the Residency. They'll talk to citizens. They'll hunt the city for me, and that's no good." He stood up, brushed off their protesting hands, even Sbi's, whose advice he valued, and walked down the steps and onto the street, parting the crowd to walk out to the Outsiders.

The colonel was one, resplendent with black plastic and weapons, like the rest of them. They had lifted the weapons when he came forward, lifted them again, because his companions had insisted on following him, and standing with him, and the crowd gathered uncertainly behind.

"Master Law," the colonel said, seeming doubtful. They had met only once, and perhaps he was much changed.

"Colonel. What do you want here?"

The colonel lifted a hand, pointed back toward the

Residency. "I don't make sense of the First Citizen, Master Law. He's alone. He refused to see us. Only he said something about *your* controlling things. That this was your doing."

Herrin regarded him sadly. "So you come to me for answers?"

"Do you have control in this city?"

"We're restoring order. Ask me, if you will ask things. I have the responsibility."

"We deal with you?"

"For convenience's sake, I think you might. I can deal with you."

The colonel frowned. "I'm not here to play logical games. I want order."

"No. Go back to the port. This is Kierkegaard. We invite you to come back this evening. I'll talk with you. There are so many things I want to learn, colonel."

The colonel looked uneasily beyond his shoulder, where Sbi stood.

"I am also," said Sbi, "curious. I shall be with Master Law."

"This evening," Herrin said.

The colonel hesitated, and then nodded, started to offer his hand and Herrin held up his, refusing the gesture with his bandages. The colonel stopped in consternation and looked confused for the moment. "Sir," the colonel said. "Where shall I find you this evening?"

"The University. Come there. You need no guns, colonel. There's no need."

"Sir," said the colonel, and, motioning to his companions, turned and walked back the way they had come.

A murmuring broke out around them. Herrin turned, saw the street jammed with people shoulder to shoulder, as far as he could see to the dome and all along the fronts of buildings. He was dazed by the sight and the relative silence with which they had come, lifted a hand to tell them it was all right.

They simply stood, not offering to disperse.

"Please," he said, "go on. Go tend things that need doing."

There was no panic rush this time. Some did as he said; some moved necessarily in his direction, but gave him a great deal of room, watching him the while. A few put out hands in his direction as if they would like to touch, or as if the gesture itself meant something.

He went to the University that night, and Sbi went, and another of the ahnit. There was Pace and Phelps, but Gytha stayed outside in view of the crowd. He had put on blue robes himself, as many did, and stood on the steps to keep matters calm.

"Come and go as you like," Herrin told the colonel. "Enter University. We honor all agreements that benefit us both, but we won't have weapons in the streets."

"What about the First Citizen?"

"He doesn't want to come out," Herrin said quietly. He had tried; himself, he had tried, but Waden stayed to his own refuge. "Someday, perhaps." They had buried Keye, with the rest of the dead that day, all in one sad grave. "We welcome visitors, colonel. But while you may have your port compound, once across that line, you're on our soil and in our State, and while we'll be hospitable, we'll issue the invitations. We take responsibility for ourselves, and for those who come here."

The colonel said nothing for a moment. Perhaps he remembered walking through that vast, quiet crowd outside.

"So," said Sbi, "do we—issue the invitations."

"That puts the matter," the colonel said, "in a special category. If there's native government."

"Oh," said Sbi, "there is."

The colonel did not stay long, even on the world itself. Outsiders came and went, silently building their station and dealing in trade.

There was a time that Herrin found it possible to walk the streets again unescorted. "Master Law," they would hail him there, and touch his sleeve very gently, with great reverence. He talked to them in the streets, and sometimes sat down on a step where half a hundred would gather to listen to him reason with them. Sometimes Sbi gathered crowds mixed of ahnit and human, or they reasoned together. Perhaps they did not all understand, but Herrin tried, at least, to use the simplest of things.

There was a path worn to the statue in the hills, and there were always humans and ahnit thereabouts; it was the tradition to walk, even when it became possible to use transport.

His parents came on the bus from Camus, and came sor-

rowfully and begged his pardon. He forgave them, even understanding that they came because he was visible again, and
people asked them about him, and they could no longer pretend him away. Sbi and Leona Pace, Gytha and Phelps and
John Ree . . . they knew him much better, and loved him,
and so it was only a little painful to regret that his parents
did not.

Harfeld died; Herrin was sorry: he would have gone to
Camus to be with the old man, who had evidently wanted
that, but it was too late when he heard the man was gone.

And finally Waden Jenks came, from his dark refuge in
the Residency, thin and blinking in the sun, and brought by
ahnit, who had finally persuaded him out. "Waden," Herrin
said, and offered him an embrace, which Waden accepted,
and looked in his eyes.

"It's not so bad, your reality," Waden confessed. "I've seen
it . . . from the windows. I thought I would come out today."

"Good," Herrin said, laid a hand on his shoulder—the
hands healed, but never quite straight—and walked with him
along the street, with Sbi and the other ahnit who had
brought him out. He let Waden choose the way he would
walk, but knew where Waden would go, ultimately.

And Waden stood in the dome, tears running down his
face while he looked at the hero-image the morning sun made
of him. There were others there, surprised by sudden visitors,
but the silence was very deep.

"There are years to come," Herrin said. "There's need of
you, Waden."

Waden looked at him, nodded slowly.

Herrin left him there, walked away with Sbi and the others, trusting that Waden would follow, in his own time.